LKJ is a world critic, guest speaker, and a live reporter. She has had many years' experience in her field, however, decided to write her novel on the loss of her mother. She has written three more novels that conclude her story so far. She hopes that her own heartache is captured by her readers and may help with their own journey through life.

LKJ believes there is a book inside everyone and perhaps this novel may offer her readers inspiration to write their own life journey.

The book is fiction-based, telling the story of the author's own life journey of loving and losing an empowering love.

This book is dedicated to my mother and to all the mothers in the world, also to cancer victims and survivors of cancer.

To my readers—always seek help for any mental health problems.

LKJ

THE BROKEN GIRL IN THE RED SHOES

AUSTIN MACAULEY PUBLISHERS™

LONDON · CAMBRIDGE · NEW YORK · SHARJAH

Copyright © LKJ (2020)

Ordering Information
Quantity sales: Special discounts are available on quantity purchases by corporations, associations, and others. For details, contact the publisher at the address below.

Publisher's Cataloging-in-Publication data
LKJ
The Broken Girl in the Red Shoes

ISBN 9781645758297 (Paperback)
ISBN 9781645758303 (Hardback)
ISBN 9781645758310 (ePub e-book)

Library of Congress Control Number: 2020920258

www.austinmacauley.com/us

First Published (2020)
Austin Macauley Publishers LLC
40 Wall Street, 28th Floor
New York, NY 10005
USA
mail-usa@austinmacauley.com
+1 (646) 5125767

**"To have been shown love so deep in your life from someone,
You will have to grieve deep to know the love was real."**

To my husband, for his daily support and love in my life.
My soul mate and best friend.
Yvonne, a woman who always supports.
Rebecca, for the many hours of friendship.
To my family and grandchildren.
Adrienne Maisel, my manager, for the constant support.

Table of Contents

Chapter 1:
Soul Searching

Charlotte stood staring out of the window in their beautiful, crisp apartment.

The apartment looked directly out at the beautiful sea and the daily cruise ships and yachts that passed by her window. She heard the sounding of the ship's horns and saw people waving from the decks to their loved ones, as they set off on their journeys.

Where were they going? Charlotte thought. So many unanswered questions, as she watched the ships sail away. She wondered too if anyone else was running away, or were they suffering like her, with deep pain and grief?

She watched the people on the beach—people who were running or walking, or maybe chatting to others who were also enjoying the freedom of the day.

Charlotte then found herself fixated on a little puppy as it played in the water. It seemed almost frightened as the waves caught it off guard.

If I had been an animal, Charlotte thought to herself, *Would my life have been similar to that of a human? Would I have had the same feelings? Would I have felt the same pain?*

Charlotte then focused back toward the sea. It, too, could become calm or erratic. The power and strength of the sea could be unleashed without notice, leaving behind either total devastation and destruction, or a feeling of complete peace and solace.

Changing images, ever evolving. Local artists were constantly trying to capture these images with each stroke of the brush.

Charles had decided to move Charlotte to the coast, and after a few months he had begun to see a slight improvement, thanks to the slow pace of life and the utter tranquility they had begun to discover.

Charlotte stared out of the window most days, not even knowing if Charles was there, but the change of scenery had started to give her some form of peace.

As for Charles, he feared for Charlotte, as he had been through this before with her, and never thought that she would survive.

Now Charlotte was destroyed inside again, her mind and body, but most of all her soul. Could he save her again, would it be possible? She had come back before, she had survived, they had moved on, learned to laugh, learned to hold each other again, whilst the pain became a distant memory.

Charles had needed to take drastic action again to save his wife. He didn't know if he could save her this time, but he was going to try. He wasn't going to give up, he couldn't lose her.

Charles had wanted Charlotte to find reflection and he had hoped he could bring her back from where she had fallen again so deeply. He had lost his faith in God, for he too couldn't understand why life was dealing them such cruel blows. Why, when there was so much love, why, when Charlotte had recovered, would she be dealt yet another devastating life changing blow? One that could surely see his beautiful wife, his love, his soul mate, taken away from him. He had to fight, he was the power, the only force against God, the only one who could fight for Charlotte, as she herself was too weak to fight any more.

Charles would scream loudly, "Why?" How could anyone survive so much pain and loss? Charlotte had suffered so much.

Why, God? Charles would question in his mind.

*****

Charlotte looked toward the sky, at the sun's reflections, almost like rays of dancing light creating rainbows of color across the skyline. Clouds formed different shapes, and images appeared that seemed as familiar as a story in your mind, as you were drawn to the performance that was taking place.

"Charlotte!"

Charles called out to her, but she didn't respond to Charles, she was in another world.

Charles went back to his study. He would check on Charlotte frequently, as he had taken to working from home. He just couldn't leave her, because of what had happened all those years before. Charles had been left with his own personal scars.

Charlotte would hardly eat or drink, she just spent most of her time staring out of the window or crying to herself in her bed.

Suddenly it appeared, it was there! She could finally see the stairway!

"Thank God!"

Finally, she had found them.

"I'm coming, I'm coming, I'm on my way!" Her heart was now racing, and her mind was traveling at such speed as it drew her toward the steps, and perhaps peace, as she reached out to take the steps to heaven.

At that very moment, Charlotte felt the pain in her stomach, the depth of which, when it hit, was as if she had just taken a massive punch.

It was back—the pain, it was destroying Charlotte's soul. It was an overwhelming feeling as if she was going to fall, her body totally exhausted.

"Mum!" she cried out, "Come back! Luke! I'm here at the window, send Mum home!"

Her tears were now falling like raindrops from the sky. "Why? Please, Mum, come back!"

*****

Charlotte's mind then took her back, to the memory of her darling mother, Anne. Her mother had passed away after a short illness, unaware she was going to be taken so quickly, at the age of 66. Her darling mother Anne, the one who fought for her life, the one who gave her life. Anne was the most precious and the most wonderful mother in the world.

Anne, who had herself suffered so much emotional turmoil and heartache during her 66 years of life. Anne had now gone from Charlotte's world and seemed to have taken Charlotte's soul with her when she had drawn her last breath and died in her daughter Charlotte's arms.

Anne had been born in a beautiful small village in Sandsend on the Yorkshire coast and was one of eight children, Anne being the second youngest. Anne's mother, Florence, was a very rounded and warm mother, and her father a strong Yorkshire man who worked hard for his family. He was the master of his home, the breadwinner, and the provider. Albert worked twelve hard manual hours a day with his strong worn hands. He was a man of short build, a very handsome man with striking blue eyes.

Florence had fallen in love with him at first glance. Anne was born on February 22nd, 1948, a beautiful girl, the only girl born to Albert and Florence, a much-loved sister to the six boys they had been graced with before.

Albert and Florence felt totally blessed by God with the gift of their daughter. Albert had always known within his own heart that Florence had secretly wished for a girl. Nonetheless, they thanked God for the healthy child, whether it be a boy or a girl, and looked forward to the child becoming part of their growing family.

Anne began to grow and became a playful and happy little girl, the apple of her father's eye. She was a mini creation of her mother, Florence, always with the protective eyes of her siblings upon her.

Albert and Florence were graced with another child after Anne, a son, making him the last of Anne's siblings.

Anne's character was growing, and at six years of age, and with a very adventurous side, she decided for the first time that she would venture from the village toward the woods where the bluebells and daffodils grew.

Anne spent her time casually picking the bluebells which glistened from the morning dew. She had wandered away from the path, but Anne had no fear, nor did she know what fear felt like. Suddenly, she heard the cry of her name. Her father, brothers, and almost the whole village appeared in front of her eyes.

Anne had lost track of time and had been reported missing from the village. For almost seven long, painful hours, they had desperately searched for her through the deep woods. She had been found safe and unharmed. Anne was chastised severely, though never did she feel the hand of her father. Albert's strict words were enough, and from that day onwards, Anne was never allowed to leave the village until she was 16.

Albert's sister, Mary, had been taken poorly and was needing assistance. Anne's mother, Florence, was still needed at home she now had eight strong men to feed.

Mary no longer lived in the village where she had been brought up. She had married a coal miner and relocated at the age of 23 to South Wales. Mary's husband had unfortunately died in an awful mine disaster nine years later, leaving her a widow who had chosen not to remarry.

Albert was now Mary's next of kin, for Mary and her husband had not been fortunate to be gifted with children.

Albert put a log on the open fire and sat back in his chair, a rustic old rocker with a thick, rugged wooden frame. Florence placed the blanket that she had knitted him one

Christmas over his knees. Albert started rocking in his chair, pondering how he was going to deal with this situation. Deep in thought, he began rocking back and forth as he lit his pipe several times. The smoke began making small circles in the air, as he drew in the tobacco. Albert turned to Florence. Her eyes immediately filled with tears, and she felt her stomach churn. Florence knew instantly what Albert was about to suggest before he had even begun to speak the words.

"Here is the case, my dear, we have no choice but to send Anne to help look after Mary. She needs our help, and Anne will care and nurse Mary back to good health. God is seeking our help, Florence!"

They were a strongly religious family, who always adhered to the word of God.

"Albert, Anne knows nothing in the world other than this village!"

"Florence, my dear! Jack will take Anne, and God will return her back to us in no time!"

As the morning chorus began, Anne felt the covers move and the warmth of her mother's voice, "Wake up, Anne, you need to get dressed!"

"Why, Mother?"

"Jack has to take you to Wales to care for Auntie Mary. She has become quite poorly, and is needing your help, darling, to care for her, and to help her overcome her sickness."

"Really, Mother! Really?"

Anne was surprised but almost overwhelmed, she had always been curious about what lay beyond the village.

As Anne was leaving, she turned back toward the gate as she heard her mother's voice,

"Be careful, darling!"

Anne left with her brother Jack, carrying her father's suitcase and her mother's hat and handbag. She was feeling very grown-up.

"Come on, Jack!"

"Anne, now you listen to me, young lady, it is a scary place beyond our village, you must take care, and follow Father's clear instructions!"

"Yes, Jack, I hear you! Come on, Jack, the train is here!"

Chapter 2:
Auntie Mary

The train pulled into the small station. Anne and Jack opened the carriage door. It looked very similar to her village. It had the same smells—and still the same amount of sheep, Anne giggled to herself. Although she couldn't help noticing that the sky was grey, like a thick dark smog that clothed the landscape.

Tiny flint cottages nestled among the valleys, and streams ran down the stone strewn hills that lay behind.

Anne and Jack arrived at the Keeper's cottage. Albert had given Jack instructions that the key would be under the mat. Mary was too frail to open the door, but Anne had been assured that it was a tiny, yet safe village and that Dr. John Andrews would be calling every day, so she was not to worry.

Dr. Andrews was a wealthy 42-years-old, the son of a lord, whose parents owned a stately home in the very next village; a stately home that sat amongst five hundred and 50 acres of prime land.

Jack called out to Auntie Mary as they entered the cottage into the small lounge where she sat, looking extremely frail. *She had such a sweet essence about her; so different*, Anne thought, *from her father*.

"Hello, Auntie Mary, I am Anne!"

"Our dear, Anne!"

At that very moment, Anne felt at ease. Anne had not let on to either Jack or her family, that she had actually been feeling very apprehensive.

Jack had a cup of tea and a sandwich but had to get back to the station, as he had a long journey back to Yorkshire. He hugged Anne and reminded her to write weekly with updates on Auntie Mary's progress as per his father's instructions.

Jack, although the youngest, was the one who Anne was supposed to be in control of. She would remind him of this fact often, but in reality, it turned out that being a girl, whether older or not, didn't matter, as the younger brother would still be in charge.

The joys of being a girl! she thought so many times. Anne set to work in Keeper's cottage, looking after Auntie Mary. When the clock on the mantelpiece chimed six o'clock, Anne looked out of the window, awaiting Dr. Andrew's first daily visit.

At that time of the evening, the lights would begin to flicker in the distance from the cottages around, as the day turned to night. Luckily, Anne was never spooked by the dark, or by the unknown. Coming from the Yorkshire Dales, she knew nothing different, and this village wasn't so dissimilar from her own.

Then she heard the creaking sound of the iron gate, as the shadow of a tall gentleman approached Keeper's cottage.

A firm hard knock of the heavy black knocker on the door seemed to make Anne jump out of her skin at that moment. Anne had never felt a nervous uneasiness in her stomach before; this was a completely different feeling from her apprehension in leaving her family.

She opened the door. There he stood, approximately six feet tall, with a handsome rugged face that almost knocked Anne to the floor. Anne's cheeks blushed.

What on earth is going on? she asked herself, *Why am I having these feelings?*

All she knew was that this was a completely different experience from anything she had felt before.

"Hello, you must be Dr. Andrews!"

"Indeed, and you must be Anne?"

Dr. Andrews continued his daily visits, and before Anne knew it, three months had gone by. At this time, Auntie Mary was now back up on her feet.

Anne had made friends with some local people in the village whilst picking up the groceries from the local store. She had written home weekly, as per her father's request, and received warm letters back, telling of life in her own village. Florence was missing her daughter so much, her presence and laughter in the home, but she never let on how deeply she missed her to Anne.

One evening, Dr. Andrews arrived promptly as usual.

"Well, Mary, you are indeed back in fine health, so, unfortunately, our daily visits will now come to an end. It has been my pleasure to visit and help you to recover your health—you had me a little worried for a time. However, your niece has been an excellent nurse, and has made my job so much easier."

"Thank you, Dr. Andrews, she is a blessing from God! I am so grateful my brother could help me in sending Anne!"

Dr. Andrews had in fact extended his visits for longer than was necessary, as an excuse to see Anne. In fact, Dr. John Andrews had secretly and deeply fallen in love with Anne, although he had never so much as laid a simple kiss on her sweet, beautiful, pure, innocent lips. Over the last three months he had watched her quiet dedication to Mary, and unknown to Anne, he had been looking out for her from his surgery window whenever she visited the local store.

"Dr. Andrews, thank you again for your visits, and thank you also to my precious Anne, you have helped me to regain my health, and I'm grateful to you both!"

"Mary, I wonder if I may, with your permission, of course, take Anne out for an evening, to thank her personally for her help and dedication. She has been quite the little nurse and has made my job so much easier."

Mary looked across to Anne to see how she would react.

"Anne, darling, how do you feel about that my dear, would you like to go? Would you feel comfortable?"

Anne was so quiet and softly spoken, not to mention extremely shy. But Mary had her answer—Anne's face had reddened with bashfulness.

"Yes, I would like that very much, thank you, Dr. Andrews, for your kind gesture," she smiled.

Dr. Andrews agreed to collect Anne on Saturday at six o'clock. Dr. Andrews' parents were throwing a dinner and dance for the locals, as a thank you for their help in bringing in the harvest, and he wanted to take Anne as his guest.

Anne was very anxious, as she knew only a few local people. This was all new territory for her, completely out of her normal domain. Anne wore her only dress, a plain grey one, which was a little crumpled and worn. She then brushed her long black hair. Anne didn't wear makeup; she had a natural beauty, a gift bestowed on her from her parents' genes.

The knock came at six o'clock as usual. Dr. Andrews was a man of precision.

"Hello, Anne, I must say how lovely you are looking this evening!"

She smiled shyly back at him.

"Thank you, Dr. Andrews!"

"Anne, please call me John, I am no longer calling in a professional manner!"

"Enjoy your evening, Anne, dear, a pretty sight you look indeed!" called Mary, as John replied, "I will have her back to you by half past eleven—and thank you, Mary, I will take great care of her!"

Anne was extremely nervous, but John took control and guided her through the evening. He introduced her to his rather stuffy parents. Anne had impeccable manners, and despite her shyness, she spoke warmly to his parents, his friends, the staff, and the local villagers.

Anne and John never took their eyes off each other all evening.

Chapter 3:
Mixed Blessings

Six months had passed since their first evening together, and they had become inseparable.

Anne had written to her father and mother telling them all about John, and of course, they had written to Auntie Mary for more details. Her father and mother approved of the courtship, even though the age gap between them was large.

"Anne, darling, I am so sorry I am late, my last patient, dear Mrs. McIntyre, could talk for Wales!"

Anne laughed. "John, your work has to come first, I don't mind how late you are!"

"Anne, I have told my parents that we shall be late joining them for dinner this evening."

"John, is everything OK? You look worried, I can see it in your eyes."

"My dear, Anne, always worrying about me, how could I ever be worried about you in my life? I have everything I have ever wished for. I may be older than you, yet you seem so much wiser than me, especially when it comes to dealing with blood!" he laughed. Anne had become quite the little nurse and helper at his surgery.

"John, don't, you'll make me blush again, you know how I do that!"

"Come on, Anne, let's go, have you brought your willies, darling?"

"Yes, John!"

That was the only thing that irritated Anne regarding John. He was a man of precision and liked to have order in his life, whereas Anne was a person of free spirit and will. She never worried about things, life was for living, as far as she was concerned.

"Are the salmon coming up the stream yet, John, is it time? I do love coming to watch the salmon—especially when you fall in the stream!" Anne was overcome with a fit of giggles.

John was at his best with Anne, when he seemed free of work and the pressures that daily life entailed. Anne had shown John a new kind of freedom with their shared adventures over the last six months, and she had unleashed a side within him that he never knew existed.

Anne's infectious personality just grew, and John's heart opened up to experience a love he had never known before in all his years.

"Anne, you really are quite a minx on the quiet! Where has that little girl gone? The shy, bashful girl that first opened the door to me? The day I fell madly in love with you, Anne—although you looked like a startled rabbit in the headlights. I actually thought you might be the patient and not your Auntie Mary!"

"I was a little overwhelmed when I opened the door to you! John, did I just hear you correctly, did you just say that you love me?"

"Your sweet innocence, alongside your unconditional love is why, yes, Anne, I have fallen in love with you."

Tears began to fall from her eyes as she told of her own deep love and how she never wanted to live a day without him by her side. In fact, their worlds had actually, joined and become complete.

"Anne, come on, let's go and watch the salmon lay their eggs."

They walked hand in hand toward the riverbank, to where the salmon came to spawn. The noise of the rushing river was running through their ears, and the spray was forming prancing white horses. Both of them stood and marveled at the magnificent skills of the salmon. They discussed their fraught and dangerous journey from the ocean, hundreds of miles away, back to the fresh waters of their birthplace—a long and dangerous journey which each salmon undertakes so that they in turn can spawn.

"John, can you see them?"

Like flying iridescent arrows, the salmon leaped across the water, grazing the surface like hunters, to make their last journey back to the home where they hatched as an alevin. Each salmon was intent on trying to reach its destiny and lay its spawn.

Anne, at that moment, saw a very strange look in John's eyes.

"John, you look like you have seen a ghost!"

"Anne, some of these salmon have come from the Atlantic, but a rare few have come all the way from the Pacific Ocean. Do you understand what happens to a salmon after they have spawned?"

"No, John, I don't, you are scaring me!"

"Anne for a Pacific salmon, this is their time to die. Once they have spawned, their destiny has been fulfilled. Anne, please stand up!"

"John, what is going on?"

"I have a life-changing question to ask you, Anne. You must listen very carefully and understand what I am saying."

"Just tell me, John, please!"

"Anne, will you be my wife, my equal, to love each other until we take our last breath? But before you give your answer, there is a promise you must make and keep!"

"John, of course, I will, I understand the confidentiality of your patients, and the trust, loyalty, and privacy both of your work and your parents' estate."

John hesitated, "Anne, unlike these salmon, who are happy to spawn and then to die, I don't want to ever spawn, I don't ever want to have children. If you marry me, no children will be born from us. Do you understand this, Anne? I have no room in my heart or mind, I only have my love for you. I cannot share it. I will walk away brokenhearted and live a life alone, with just the memory of you in my heart and mind. This is the condition of my hand of marriage."

John's heart was now pounding, his eyes began filling with tears, could this be the end? Had he already fulfilled his life with just the love of Anne or was the answer now to be, "No?" For then his heart would die.

Anne had tears in her eyes, and her heart was also pounding inside, what was she going to do? Her whole childhood had been in the warmth of her beautiful family, whereas John came from a family that didn't touch, or show any emotion. The only emotional love he knew was from Anne.

"John," she began, as tears started to fall from her beautiful blue eyes.

Anne had never cried in front of John; John had never given any reason to make her cry.

"How can I live without you? I don't even know what it would be like to be a mother…!"

Anne paused, thoughts spinning around her mind.

"John, could you prevent this from happening, is there a way to stop it?"

"Of course, it would be my duty and honor to prevent it."

"I agree then, John, and accept your hand of marriage." John and Anne embraced each other.

As the salmon continued their journey upstream to the gravel beds, passers-by reflected on the beautiful picture in front of them, of two lovers embracing. Little did they know that the lovers were soon to become husband and wife, but in a marriage with mixed blessings.

Chapter 4:
The Red Shoes

John stood at the altar, looking extremely handsome, but for the first time in his life, he was feeling anxious. The chapel pews were filled to the brim. Florence was sitting with her seven sons and some of their wives, awaiting the arrival of Anne through the church doors on her father's arm.

Florence had helped dress Anne, reflecting how beautiful she looked in the gown she had spent so many hours toiling over.

John's parents and distant relatives were sitting in the pews next to where John was standing. Anne's relatives, friends and local villagers filled the remaining pews.

Albert looked at his beautiful daughter as they stood outside the church.

"Anne, you look stunning, and you remind me of the day that I married your mother."

"Thank you, Father," and she gently placed a kiss upon his cheek.

"Anne, we hope you're blessed with a beautiful family, the most precious gift from God."

Anne's heart sank, she dared not tell her father of the promise she had made with John, on accepting his hand of marriage. As unto God's Holy Law, to use any form of contraception was regarded as a sin, and one against their religion.

Anne had forsaken the right to bear children for John's love. Her father and mother would never have allowed the marriage to go ahead if they had known. This would be an act against God. John would have been seen as a man of great sin.

"I have to learn to be a wife first, Father," she said, brushing away his comment.

"Anne, are you sure this is what you want? Although you have chosen your path, it is not too late to change your mind?"

"Father, Mother will wonder what's happening, and John will think I'm not coming either!"

"Well, Anne, I have my answer."

The priest then appeared at the church door.

"Albert, Anne, is everything OK?"

"Indeed, it is Father, I was just checking on my daughter before we entered the house of our Lord."

The priest then gave a little wink to Albert. He had become quite used to protective fathers standing outside the church on many occasions.

"Ready, Father!"

Anne linked her arm into his and they entered the doors of the church.

The organist began. Anne slowly and calmly walked down the aisle, carefully taking each step. She could hear the gasps as she glided down the aisle in her beautiful dress, which was adorned with lace created by her mother's hands.

Anne was simply a vision as the sun's rays shone through the stained-glass windows. She wore a veil shielding her face, and a heavy white satin gown, with a boat neckline that fitted neatly on her delicate frame.

Albert held his head high as they approached the altar.

John could not hide his delight at seeing her, he simply couldn't refrain from gently whispering, "You look amazing."

Anne gave a very shy and bashful look back to him, as they exchanged the wedding vows, followed by the exchange of rings.

The church bells rang out across the valley. As the church doors opened, Anne and John were now husband and wife.

The day seemed to pass so quickly, from the formal photographs, which were taken with a simple Brownie camera, to Anne and John's first dance. Albert sang alongside Anne's brothers and local villagers. It sounded like a choir, with the beautiful sounds that the men made as their voices echoed through the Welsh valley.

John was now extremely merry. Anne had never seen him this way, but then again, he had never had an evening drinking with her father and brothers. They really could drink all those many jugs of ale with no problems! Sometimes they would fall off their chairs, as she remembered happening many evenings in her childhood.

Her brother Peter appeared. He was driving Anne and John to their new marital home, a stunning little flint cottage on the private estate of John's parents. They would now live in the magnificent grounds, where the huge mansion took precedence over the landscape set amongst the many acres of prime land. John had asked Anne her thoughts on whether to live in the mansion or the cottage. He was extremely happy when she said the cottage, as he had always found the house so daunting.

"Come on, John, let's get you indoors!"

"Anne, I feel like I could dance all night."

"John, you need to go to bed, darling!"

"Ahh, Anne, darling, where at last I can finally hold you, and take you as my wife."

Anne entered the bedroom of what was now their matrimonial home. She suddenly started to feel a little apprehensive. Her mother's description of what happened to girls was going through her mind. When she had told Anne about the events that would happen when she changed from a girl to a young lady, she had explained that her monthly cycle would only stop when she was carrying a child. Her mother had then followed up with a rather matter of fact explanation on how a child was produced by a man and a woman.

Anne looked around the room, the reality of her mother's conversation in her head, with no idea of what or how to do this realistically. *John had had quite a lot to drink*, she thought, *and hopefully he might never notice her lack of experience in this department.* Suddenly, Anne's eyes were drawn to a box on the bed, as John entered the bedroom rather clumsily.

"Anne, darling, open the box!"

The most amazing red shoes dazzled back at her.

"John, they're simply beautiful!"

"They were my grandmother's shoes! She was a beautiful dancer, Anne, and we shall dance our journey of life together, as did she!"

John then slowly started to undo Anne's dress, fumbling a little with the zip, the moon's glow revealing her beautiful, soft, delicate skin. He gently kissed her back as her dress dropped to her waist. She stood holding onto him, and she could suddenly feel the firmness of his torso. Her dress fell to the floor. She nervously started undoing the buttons on his shirt, as he helped her and let it fall to the floor. The masculinity of his firm chest, her hands trembling, not quite sure what to do. John unbuckled his belt and removed his trousers, then began to kiss Anne's body, their bodies now reacting to each other as they caressed. Only the moonlight glow was lighting the room as John took her hand and led Anne gently to their bed. Anne and John made love to each other and became one.

"Oh, John!" Anne groaned. She was full of ecstasy, her body trembling with every touch, and as he entered her again, she was now exhausted in passion.

"Morning, darling!" just as the sun came through the window, "would you like some breakfast?"

"Mrs. Andrews, the only thing I want is you."

Six weeks had passed since their wedding, and John was being very careful to protect the promise that they had entered into before their marriage.

"John, I am not feeling very well. Do you mind if I stay in bed this morning? I am a little exhausted."

"You do look a little pale, darling."

John arrived home late that evening. A torrid wave of sickness had ripped through half the village.

John leaned over and kissed Anne.

"I come bearing warm soup! Mrs. Jones sends her regards. She swears by this recipe, and it will help you regain your strength."

"John, I am so sorry, some wife I am! I can't even get a meal ready for when you come in from working so hard!"

And her tears began to fall.

"Anne, there is no need to cry, you haven't failed any wifely duties, in fact, perhaps I have pushed your wonderful body too far. Come here, let's wipe those tears away. Now, you're not alone either, there is a terrible virus going around the village."

Anne hugged John tight, she was quite tearful.

"I just felt like such a failure lying here, John."

It was now a beautiful July evening and their March wedding seemed a lifetime ago. Anne was settling into her role as Mrs. Andrews.

"Anne, come on! Are you ready darling? Mother and father will be waiting."

"OK, John! I am coming, I can't get the zip up on this dress, I need your help—and look at granny's red shoes with my outfit, John, don't they look beautiful!"

"Anne, breathe in, let me try this zip." After a little help and pulling, the zip went up.

John and Anne arrived at his parent's house just before the party began. John's parents greeted them in their normal, rather cold fashion. His parents thought they were greeting them warmly, as they knew of no other way.

The party was a huge affair, with around two hundred guests, and took place in their stunning banqueting hall.

It was almost 11 o'clock when Anne heard John's voice calling to her.

"Anne! It's OK, you fainted darling!" Anne was lying on the ground quite dazed.

"The ambulance is on its way, darling, don't worry, I'm here."

The ambulance journey seemed to take forever. John's mind was in overdrive, *I should have noticed something how could I have missed this, Anne being sick?*

The ambulance suddenly stopped as the doors flew open, the sound of the trolley wheels whisking Anne through the corridor of the emergency center, John running closely behind.

"It's OK, Dr. Andrews, we'll take it from here."

"Anne, darling, I'm just outside, I love you."

The clock on the wall seemed to tick forever. He paced up and down the corridor as the surgeon came through the door. He removed his mask and started to remove his blood-stained gloves.

"Dr. Andrews?"

"Yes, is Anne OK? How did I miss the fact that she was sick? I am a doctor after all!"

"John—may I call you John?"

"Yes, of course."

"Please take a seat, John. Anne is suffering from concussion. Your wife hit her head rather hard when she fainted, she is going to feel very sore for a little while. I have no doubt you will be there to ensure she gets back on her feet."

"Of course, she is my wife, my world!"

John rose to his feet, as the doctor continued.

"Well, John, in five months' time your wife's Christmas present will be one for the rest of your life. You will have the gift of a beautiful child. Anne is pregnant, that's why she fainted—and she was a little dehydrated too."

"What did you just say?"

"Dr. Andrews, you are going to be a father! Most fathers look like you, John, a lot of them have that same look when they are told!"

John's face grew increasingly horrified, as the doctor continued to look at him.

"I will give you a few minutes to absorb it all, it's a lot to take in, your wife fainting, and hurt, and then finding out you are going to be a father."

The surgeon then explained that Anne was very sleepy, and that rest was what she needed.

John paced up and down the corridor, his hands on his face.

"Why, why, how did this happen? How could this have happened to us? I have done everything possible to prevent this!"

His promise to Anne had been that he would ensure that she would never carry a child, it had been for him to deal with that side of things. A child, a fetus, was now growing, and it was already 14 weeks old.

Then John remembered the night of their wedding. He had drunk far too much and was completely blown away by the passion of Anne. How naïve she had been, a virgin, he had led her to the bed to ease her trembling.

He had caressed her body, and then—suddenly John remembered that he had forgotten to put on the protective sheath. *How could he have been so irresponsible?* John's mind was going over and over everything, *and how he could solve this?*

The answer, for him, was not hard to find. He remembered that the law had changed, and abortions were now legal. Anne would have to have the child aborted, that had been their agreement; no children.

When John walked into the room, Anne looked straight at him like a little lost child.

"John, I'm so sorry, I'm so sorry, I don't know how it happened!"

"It's OK darling, it was my fault, it was completely my fault. Please don't fret darling, we will get through this, and I will sort it. I promised you that it was my responsibility to make sure this didn't happen, but I will take care of the situation now. I'm so sorry that I have caused you this pain."

John then leaned over and kissed Anne on her lips.

"Now you need to rest, darling, and I will be here by your side whilst you sleep; it will all be different in the morning."

"I love you, John!"

The drugs had now kicked in and Anne was sleeping.

John quietly crept out of the room to find her doctor in charge. After a long, heated conversation with him, John ordered Anne's abortion to happen when she awoke in the morning. He wouldn't allow time or even consideration, he simply repeated that Anne would have the fetus removed in the morning. He was in charge, she had given him the right, and now he had to follow this through. Anne would not be a mother, the fetus had to go. It was not a child in the eyes of the law until 24 weeks, it was simply a fetus. She had entered the agreement of her own free will when she could have walked away, but she had chosen John and their life ahead.

"It had to go," the words that John had carved in his mind, as a coldness overcame him, he was the decider it was his right, Anne had given him control as part of their agreement. John pausing for a moment with his thoughts, as he stood outside Anne's room in the hospital corridor.

At that very moment, a young gentleman walked past him, wondering what on earth had happened. He looked at John with his own thoughts and wondering if the poor man had just been told of the death. Yet, if he could have read John's mind, or heard the conversation he had had with Anne's doctor, he would have thought you cruel, cold-hearted bastard!

*****

The room was set, ready to abort the fetus that had come from the first night of their marriage, their first night of holding and touching each other's bodies. Now in this room, a grown woman lay, a woman who was no longer a virgin, who was now about to face the consequences of their passion.

A consequence that would come down to her, it would be Anne actually to decide, if she was going to let this happen. Should she keep the agreement? Should she let them take this child, this unborn fetus from her womb?

Anne's head was spinning, she could hear John talking to the doctors and the clanging noises in the room. The nurses were preparing the instruments to take the fetus away.

The doctor then placed a green gown over Anne's body. He was going to put a cannula in her right hand to add the anesthetic. He explained she would have to count down when he started to put the medication in. He told Anne it would be over very quickly.

Suddenly she could hear her mother's voice in her head,

"Anne, my darling, come home, Anne, come home!"

Her mind was then telling her, *He will love the child, he will, I'm sure!* Her head was now spinning.

"No, no, but I promised him!" Her heart was pounding. Suddenly she screamed out.

"No! Stop, please, I can't, I can't let you take my child, our child, John! Please John, please, you had room in your heart for me, surely you will love the child like you have loved me!"

"Anne!" he yelled, with such fierceness in his voice, his face filled with rage, turning a deep shade of red.

"We had an agreement!"

"I know, John, but it wasn't my fault."

"I know!" he screamed back at her.

The doctor interrupted.

"—Mr. Andrews, this isn't helping, perhaps some other time?"

John looked directly at Anne.

"Now you have to decide, Anne, just like on the river bank."

"John, please, I can't!"

"Then I'm sorry, my darling, goodbye."

John turned his back and walked out of the room.

The doctor ran after John. He battled with him, telling him that perhaps he had made a decision too quickly, that time could, maybe, give a different conclusion.

But despite his efforts, the doctor failed. He could not bring John Andrews back to Anne. He was gone.

John informed the hospital a few days later that he would write to Jack to come and collect Anne. Her doctor had informed them that she would have to stay in the hospital for two weeks to recover from her fall.

John wasn't going to change his mind. He felt that Anne could have saved their marriage, but now it was over. Now he had to live with a broken heart, a life empty and alone. He could not live a life which meant he would have to share Anne with another person, so he decided that he would live now as a widower as if his wife had died. He felt as if she had indeed died, as his heart still ached and longed for her. But they as a couple had died, their love was gone. The fetus had broken their love.

Two weeks passed. The grief of losing John had taken its toll on Anne. The desperation and hope that John would come back haunted her each time the ward door opened. Had he returned? Her heart would be beating fast, had he found somewhere in his heart for them to carry on? Somewhere in his heart for their child, too, who was created from their passion and undying love?

Anne ate very little.

"You must eat, my dear." The nurse was trying every day to encourage her. Broken and weak, her pain was ripping slowly at her heart.

"You must try, Mrs. Andrews; the baby needs your strength to grow."

With that, the door opened. It was her brother Jack.

"Jack!" she cried out, her tears running down her face.

"What on earth has happened, Anne? Father received a letter from John, saying you were in the hospital and needed to go home, and that you would need our help. I had to call at the cottage to collect your personal belongings. When I arrived, there was just a note saying that you would explain everything at the hospital!"

Anne noticed that Jack was carrying her red shoes—the beautiful shoes John had given her on her wedding night.

She started to cry and began to explain everything to Jack.

"Bastard! Bloody bastard, I will knock ten barrels out of him, Anne, the coward, how dare he abandon you! How dare he treat you like this? Wait till father and mother hear!"

"Jack, my heart is broken."

Jack looked straight into Anne's eyes.

"Now you listen to me. Anne, there is a heart growing inside of you, and your own heart will mend. You have to be strong now, you're no longer a young naïve girl, you're a woman, and you must protect your child now, Anne!"

Chapter 5:
New Beginnings

Jack opened the door to their family home where Anne had been sleeping for days. Her mother had been bringing her fresh soup and bread and checking on her constantly. Florence saw that her poor child was totally lost and confused. The family was becoming increasingly worried about her and her unborn child.

Anne was now 21 weeks pregnant, and that evening, she began to bleed. Florence told Albert to fetch the doctor immediately. She was desperately worried as Anne was very weak and dehydrated, and there was every chance she could lose her child.

The doctor told them that the next 24 hours were critical. They thanked Dr. James, and he said he would call again in the morning.

Florence spoke to Albert, saying that it was time that she went in and stayed by Anne's side. It was a time for mother and daughter—she wasn't pushing Albert out, she said, but Albert knew his wife well, and knew what she had to do.

Florence lay beside Anne. She held her little girl close, for she was still her little girl. She spoke very quietly but with her warm motherly tone.

"I'm here, Anne, and whatever happens, it will be God's will. He will decide tonight if you're to be forgiven for the sin that was made with John."

Anne started to cry, she had hardly any strength left, and her body was now exhausted.

"I'm sorry, Mother, I have sinned, I know. I only thought about love, I didn't think about being a mother."

"Darling, the power of love can do many things."

"Mother, when I was in the operating room, I heard you calling for me to come home. Just as they were getting ready to take away my child, I couldn't do it mother, I couldn't— but now I have lost John."

"Anne, God created man, then woman, and He is the forgiver of all sins. God will see deep in your heart and know if you will love your child. He will decide if you have the strength to protect your child. Close your eyes and talk to God, Anne, make your peace. I will be here by your side."

Florence didn't sleep much at all. If Anne were to have a miscarriage, she could hemorrhage and die, but she didn't want to scare Anne with the details. Her journey so far had already been such an emotional one.

When Anne awoke, her mother was still by her side. Doctor James called, and gave Anne a thorough examination, telling her that she was still carrying her child. She was weak, but out of danger. Anne was to be on complete bed rest for the next six weeks to regain her strength. Tears of joy ran throughout Florence and Albert's home at the news that they were still to be grandparents.

Albert told the rest of the family that it was in Anne's best interest if John's name was never mentioned again.

As far as the family was concerned, Dr. John Andrews was now a ghost to them, it was he who had died that night, and not his child. It would be him that would pay the price to God, and he would never get to know his own child. Weak as she was, Anne agreed.

December was here—this was Anne's favorite time of the year, although she was walking around not knowing what to do with herself.

"Mother, can I help you put the decorations on the tree?"

"If you like, Anne, darling."

"It looks like we are going to have snow tonight, Mother."

Would it be a white Christmas after all? You could almost smell the snow in the air. The Yorkshire Dales looked amazing in winter.

"Your father has gone off with Jack, they're getting more firewood in, we could be in for a few difficult days. The weather looks set to hit hard."

Albert would also be out collecting a barrel of ale. He loved his family and the Christmas festivities, and he and his sons loved to celebrate with plenty of ale. As Anne stretched to place the little angel on the tree, she suddenly let out a huge cry.

"Anne, come down right now! You need to get on the bed, darling, I don't know about the snow coming, but it looks like our grandchild is!"

Anne's waters had broken, and the child was going to enter the world today. Florence calmly collected fresh towels and hot water as she headed toward Anne's bedroom. The pain of labor had started to take its toll, as her mother tried to ease the strain. Florence kept advising Anne to breathe as she gently wiped her forehead.

Three hours passed, and Anne was now fully dilated. Florence had given birth to eight children and was aware that it wouldn't be long now.

Albert and Jack came through the back door, their arms loaded down with logs. They then suddenly heard Anne's screams.

"Albert, is that you?" Florence cried out. "Call for the midwife!"

"I will go, Father, I am faster!" Jack insisted.

The whole village was looking forward to the arrival of the unborn child. The local people felt sorry for Anne—they saw her as a young girl who was now a widow in mourning and expecting a child.

Albert had spent many hours making the child a crib. His hands had been kept busy creating a beautiful masterpiece, as he and Florence awaited the arrival of their first grandchild.

Albert went to his shed to bring in the hand-carved crib ready for Anne's child. Soon God would gift them with their beautiful grandchild! His eyes began to fill with tears. Albert knew there would also be a difficult journey ahead for Anne and her child. Anne had no husband, she was alone carrying her child. John Andrews was gone, dead like the salmon he had talked about, the salmon that faced certain death after spawning.

The hours passed, and Albert and Jack paced the floors of their home. The snow had fallen, and a magical winter's scene looked back at Albert through the window as they waited. Jack placed more logs on the fire, while Albert drew on his pipe rather pensively.

Suddenly there was a cry, the sound of Anne's child as she entered her world from God's world.

"Anne, you have a beautiful baby girl, she weighs six pounds, seven ounces, and she has raven black hair!"

The time was now 2.26 a.m. on the 22nd of December 1968.

Anne was totally exhausted; the birth had taken its toll on her body. Florence carried over her beautiful gift from God, placing her in Anne's arms.

"There you go, darling, meet your daughter!"

"Oh, Mother, she is so beautiful, my little girl, my darling, little girl!"

Her tears were falling, and a teardrop fell on her child's forehead. Anne wiped the teardrop as she looked at her daughter.

"You are the most precious and beautiful little girl in the whole world, and I am your mother. I will be there for you every single day of your life. I shall teach you to dance in the rain, I will be there to catch you if you ever fall, my darling."

With that, she held the baby up.

"Charlotte, say hello to your grandmother!"

Florence's eyes filled with tears, and she was overcome with emotion.

"Anne, darling, I'm so very proud of you!"

The door knocked, and with that Albert came in,

"Anne darling, may I come in and meet my grandchild?"

Albert took the small child from Anne's arms, cradling her in his own.

"I'm your grandpapa, and you are just as beautiful as your mother was when I held her in my arms. I make you this promise too, Charlotte, I will, as long as I am on this earth, protect you."

Albert, too, was filled with emotion and tears, as Jack entered the room and rejoiced in the gift of Charlotte.

Not a single thought of John had entered Anne's mind.

John Andrews was gone. Charlotte was hers, and no one was ever taking this love away.

Chapter 6:
Confetti and Ashes

The church was full of Sunday worshippers. And Charlotte's christening was taking place during the Sunday service. Jack, along with Anne's brother Maurice and his wife Pat, had been chosen as godparents.

Charlotte was now three months old.

"Come on!" Anne shouted toward her father.

"Anne, I'm coming!"

"Father, you know how irate Father Ralph gets, you're always the last one into the church!"

Charlotte was dressed in Anne's christening gown, which had in fact been Florence's christening gown. A beautiful service had taken place, and baby Charlotte was commended as being one of a few who hadn't cried at the font. As Father Ralph baptized her, he told the congregation she would be a blessed child.

"Anne, come here, I want you to meet someone."

"Jack, what are you up to?" she protested, as Jack introduced her to a gentleman.

He had a rather rugged appearance about him and was around five years older than her. "Do you remember Robert Hughes? He used to tease you all the time at school!"

"I can't say that I do."

"Hello, Anne, what a beautiful girl you have!"

"The most precious gift I have in the world."

"As beautiful as her mother, I would say!"

"Ahh, now, Robert, flattery will get you nowhere!"

How much she had grown up since her first naive love, Anne thought. She had had to face up to promises broken and make heartbreaking decisions that could have left her without a child! She had known love but at a huge cost. A love that had cost her the loss of her husband and almost the loss of her child. From now on, no man would ever have her love like the love she had for her precious Charlotte.

It had been a wonderful day, and Charlotte's christening had been beautiful, but Anne was tired as she laid Charlotte in the crib her father had made. She thanked God for her gift again—the gift he had given her and made her fight for, with every single breath.

It wasn't too long before Charlotte began teething and seemed to be driving everyone crazy.

"Mother, I think if I take Charlotte out in the air it might do her some good?"

"Yes, Anne, perhaps the rocking of the pram might help her?"

Anne walked along the lane, thinking back to her life in the village, and the day she had got lost in the bluebell woods.

When suddenly—"Hello again!"

"Oh, hello, Robert, sorry, I was in a dream!"

"Not a lot of sleep going on then?"

"She is teething, and I don't know what to do, I feel so helpless!" Anne began to cry. She hadn't cried in months. Robert pulled out a hankie from his trouser pocket.

"Come here now, Anne, it will be OK."

He was so soft, so kind and gentle.

"May I push Charlotte? I have stronger arms than you do!" He spoke in a strong Yorkshire accent.

Anne laughed, "Oh, Robert, you're too funny! But don't push too hard though, I told you she is the most precious gift in my life!"

They walked and before they knew it, Charlotte was asleep. They had walked for a few miles, just talking.

She had talked all about her life and he had talked about his, explaining that he hadn't done anything much. He admitted to being a bit of a player with the ladies. He liked to drink with the lads, and he wanted a family, but so far, he hadn't found the right girl.

Anne wondered why he hadn't been taken before, then immediately asked herself, *why had that thought even entered her head?* She hadn't thought of any man since John, *why had he come back into her mind? She must be tired and emotional.*

"Are you OK?" The sound of Robert's voice brought her back to reality.

"Oh, Robert, I am sorry, I think I will take Charlotte back and have a sleep myself, thank you for walking with me."

"The pleasure was all mine, Anne. Maybe we can do this again?"

"Maybe!" she told him.

Life had taught her that it wasn't all fairy tales. It was very different now, and she had Charlotte to think of. Anne continued her daily walks and as the weeks passed, Robert had persevered, and Anne met him regularly. Robert had fallen for her, but he knew he couldn't rush things. Her brother Jack, her father and her mother had known that he would take his time.

"Robert, maybe we could go dancing one evening, instead of going walking one day?"

Robert looked startled.

"Oh, Robert, I'm sorry, I didn't mean to…" and she paused.

"Anne, I would love nothing more than to go dancing with you!"

"You would, Robert?"

The weeks had flown by, Robert and Anne had enjoyed many evenings dancing together, and he became part of Anne's lives. He was in love with her and Charlotte. Robert asked for Albert's permission to marry her. He declared that he would love and take care of them both and that he would love Charlotte as if she was his own flesh and blood.

Robert went down on one knee to propose to Anne, as 10-month-old Charlotte tried to crawl around the parlor room, but Anne stopped him before he could continue.

"Robert, I have to tell you something, but you must swear never to speak a word of this to anyone. I have to tell you something before I give you my answer."

"Anne, what on earth is it?"

Anne told Robert the story of John, how he had walked away from her and from their baby, and about the agreement they had both made regarding a childless marriage. She explained that when it came to the abortion, she couldn't she could not abort Charlotte. She told Robert how she had hoped John would have come to love their child, but it was not to be.

51

"Bastard, bloody bastard, what a weak coward of a man! How could any man do this?"

He totally understood why Anne's family had told everyone that John had died, to protect her and Charlotte.

"Anne, I shall be Charlotte's father. But you do know, however, that one day Charlotte will have to know?"

Suddenly, with despair in her eyes, "Why, Robert, why?"

"Because, darling, when she herself gets married, she will have to provide a birth certificate. It is the law, and she will have his name."

Anne had totally forgotten that her father had taken care of the legalities and registered Charlotte's birth.

Albert could not have put Charlotte's father down as deceased, as that would have been a crime, so John Andrew's name was on the birth certificate.

The thought of Charlotte and marriage hadn't even entered his mind. Anne flew almost into a rage; she had never raised such a tone of anger in her life.

"As far as I'm concerned, that bastard is no father, he didn't want her."

"Anne, it will be OK, I'm sure Charlotte will understand, when the time comes, don't worry, Anne."

*****

Anne and Robert were married in the chapel in their village on the 6th of April 1970, Robert beaming with pride. He was a husband and now a father, with a beautiful family. He had everything he desired in life; it was perfect.

"Robert, sit down darling, I hope work is going well at the mill?"

Robert looked at Anne rather puzzled.

"We are going to have a baby."

Robert grabbed hold of Anne and started dancing,

"Careful, Robert, you will make me sick again!"

She laughed as he picked Charlotte up from her high chair.

"You're going to have a brother or sister, my little angel, we are having a baby!"

Anne was due in January, and she was now almost eleven weeks by the doctor's count.

Robert worked hard, and he did all the overtime the mill had to offer. Anne finally had her family. Their lives were simply perfect, happy at last.

Robert came in from the mill one night after finishing a 15-hour shift.

"You look absolutely exhausted, Robert!"

"As the new manager, it's important I keep the mill running to schedule, and we need the money, Anne."

"Darling, you need time too, you need a break, why don't you go to the pub with Jack and the boys on Friday? I feel like I could do with an early evening myself, my feet are becoming a little swollen."

"Are you sure, Anne?"

"I know you don't think I'm fat, but I think I'm fatter than the turkey this year, and I still have almost eight weeks left!"

Friday came, and Anne was holding Charlotte as Robert picked up his lunch from the kitchen table.

"Daddy will be home late tonight, Mummy is going to snuggle with you and Mr. Rabbit."

"Bye, bye, Daddy!" She started blowing kisses to him from her tiny hands.

"Are you sure, darling?"

"Go on Robert, we will be fine—and try and have some fun!"

"Well, that's me told!" He laughed, then kissed Anne and Charlotte. Robert waved back at them as he walked along the road until he no longer had them in his sight.

"Mummy, Mr. Wabbit is being bad, he's hungry, Mummy!"

"Charlotte, Mr. Rabbit is being a very naughty rabbit!"

"Mummy, I want Daddy to tell him off. Daddy tell Mr. Wabbit to be a good wabbit!"

Charlotte's eyes filled with tears. She was going to be two in three weeks. She was a very bright and forward little girl.

"Charlotte, darling, be a good girl, and Mummy will tell you the story of a young girl who became a princess and wore the most beautiful red shoes that sparkled."

Anne started telling her how the princess met a frog, and when she kissed him, he became a prince. They lived happily ever after in her castle.

"Mummy, Mr. Wabbit is still hungry!"

"OK, Charlotte, I will take Mr. Rabbit and get him a carrot from the kitchen."

Later that evening, Anne looked at her watch. It was 10.20 pm. It was strange Robert not being home yet from work. Anne had become used to the pattern and also the schedule they had formed as a family.

"Damn my brother Jack!" she said aloud. Robert would be the worse for wear when he came home. It had been almost a year since he had last gone for a drink, whereas in the past, he had been a regular at the Golden Lion. But that was when he had no ties, no one to love or even care for— how different he was now that Robert was a husband and father!

Anne went back upstairs, carrying Mr. Rabbit.

Charlotte had finally fallen fast asleep. She tucked Mr. Rabbit into the blanket next to Charlotte. Anne gave her a kiss on her cheek and went to her own bed. She was tired herself and fell fast asleep almost immediately.

Anne was awoken by the sound of milk bottles rolling on the doorstep, as Robert fumbled with the keyhole.

She looked at the clock on her bedside table, it was 3.15 in the morning!

No wonder he couldn't put the key in the keyhole, she thought, as the door flew open and crashed against the wall. Anne jumped out of bed.

"For God's sake, Robert!"

She was unimpressed now because if Charlotte woke, she would be a nightmare to get back to sleep.

"Robert, sssh! Charlotte is sleeping!"

"Ahh, Anne, there you are, my beauty!"

"Come on, Robert, you need to get into bed."

His performance on the stairs was like a tap dancer on stage, then at last he arrived at the top.

"Come here, Robert, I'll help you off with your coat."

There was an overwhelming smell of perfume on him.

It hit Anne hard, as she then noticed red lipstick on the side of his face. Anne felt burning anger inside her.

She had never felt like this before. When John had walked out, she didn't feel anger, it was loss and grief, but this was different, this was betrayal.

"Robert, what the hell is this?"

"I haven't done anything, Anne, I wasn't interested, drunk or not, I'm committed to you. You're my wife, why would I do that? I am not that bastard John Andrews."

"I'm sorry, Robert, I'm sorry."

Robert angrily pulled away from Anne, as he tried to remove his coat.

"Let me help you, Robert."

"No!" He was now shouting at her. "I wish I had actually gone with that whore from the start, as clearly you doubt me, and have no faith or trust in me whatsoever."

"Robert, what was I to think?"

"Well, not that!" he shouted angrily at Anne.

"Please don't shout, you'll wake Charlotte!"

"Oh, no, I must not wake your precious Charlotte!"

Robert was now mocking her. Anne was furious.

"How dare you! Charlotte is a little girl, I will not have you mock her! Get out, Robert, until you're sober! I don't recognize the man in front of me."

Robert turned toward Anne, with his hand in full swing, and suddenly she felt a hard sting hit her face.

Anne could feel herself falling, as she screamed.

Suddenly Anne was at the bottom of the stairs with blood pouring from her mouth, and unconscious.

"Holy shit, what have I done?" Robert seemed to sober up instantly.

However, the stench from his breath would tell the tale to anyone. It was his fault. He had hit Anne, he had struck her.

"Help!" His cries falling on deaf ears, "Please somebody help!"

He then remembered that their neighbor, Mrs. Robinson, had a phone.

"Help, it's Anne, she has fallen, I think she is dead! Please can you call for an ambulance?"

"Yes, of course, go, Robert, I will be there as soon as I have called them."

Robert ran back to Anne, cradling her in his arms, sobbing, tears running from his eyes.

"Anne, what have I done? Please, God, don't let her die, or our baby!"

The ambulance arrived. It seemed to have taken a lifetime. Robert heard the sirens, then the sharp halt of the ambulance as it stopped outside with its flashing lights.

Suddenly two men appeared through the open door, one carrying paramedic equipment, the other pushing a trolley.

They asked Robert to stand aside and immediately started working on his wife.

Anne was soon on the trolley and in the ambulance. She needed to get to the hospital fast, as she was losing too much blood.

"Mr. Hughes, we need to go now, we don't have much time!"

"I need to get our daughter!"

As he turned, Charlotte was staring directly at him. She had an evil look in her eyes, almost as if she was piercing his soul, all the while holding tightly onto Mr. Rabbit.

"Charlotte, come here, darling, Mummy has had a fall, we need to go to the hospital!"

"You pushed Mummy! I saw you, and so did Mr. Wabbit! I want Mummy, I want Mummy!"

"Come here, Charlotte, I don't have time for this, we have to go and get Mummy better!" And with that he grabbed her. Charlotte began kicking and screaming again.

"Mummy!"

Robert finally got her into the ambulance, but the shock of seeing her mother like that startled her, and she sat there as if in a daze. Charlotte just stared at her mother, not knowing if she was alive or dead, holding Mr. Rabbit tightly.

The ambulance pulled up at the hospital, and Anne was whisked off to the emergency room. Robert and Charlotte were taken to the waiting room. Charlotte was still holding on tightly to Mr. Rabbit. Not a single word did Charlotte say, nor had she spoken a word since she had first seen her mother lying on the trolley.

Robert paced the room, over and over. When he eventually stopped, he sat with his head in his hands.

Before long, he was on his feet again, pacing the room, waiting for news of Anne.

Hours passed. Charlotte still sat as if she was a mannequin rather than a tiny child.

The door opened.

"Mr. Hughes, your wife is alive!"

"Thank the Lord, thank you, thank you!" Robert replied.

Then the Doctor started to explain, "Please, sit down, Mr. Hughes. Your wife is heavily sedated, and we had to perform an emergency cesarean. You have a son, Mr. Hughes."

"Oh, dear Lord, my son, our son!" exclaimed Robert.

"I'm afraid that you need to come now, Mr. Hughes, we have called for the priest. Your son, unfortunately, isn't going to survive long, maybe a few hours, and you will need this time with him. Would you like the priest to christen him?"

Robert looked at the doctor in despair. He was a broken man. God had punished him, how would he ever recover, how would they get through this, what had he done? The evil drink had destroyed him, he had broken his wife, his daughter, and now he had killed his own son.

"The nurse will stay with Charlotte," explained the doctor, as Robert walked alongside him toward a side room. Robert hesitated as he drew a deep breath and walked in.

Anne lay motionless as he bent over and kissed her mouth. Robert then gently placed his hands on her head, as tears fell from his face, and onto hers.

"Oh, my darling Anne, I'm so sorry, I am so sorry," as Anne who was only slightly coherent quietly replied,

"You name him, Robert, and remember his name. Look at our son and see how you have taken his life. I will never forgive you, Robert, never."

Anne drifted back into a deep sleep, as she had been heavily sedated. She had taken such a severe blow to her head and had lost so much blood; the doctors had been very concerned that the shock would kill her. The overwhelming concern for Anne was that she had lost her child.

Robert walked over to the crib. There he lay, their son.

He looked so perfect, so tiny and fragile. Not a sound did the child make in the stillness of the night. Robert's eyes again filled with tears, almost as if his heart was bleeding through his eyes. He gently lifted their son into his arms, cradling him next to his heart. Robert could not conceal his tears, crying as he looked at their son.

"My son, my precious boy, I'm so sorry!" he cried.

He looked up to the ceiling and spoke aloud, "Please, God, take me, not my child, please punish me, not Anne or our family!"

Robert held the small child and named him Jacob.

"Jacob, you will be forever in my heart, and I promise that I will never forget you. I will spend the rest of my life trying to make it right for your mummy, and whatever God throws at me, I shall take without complaint."

There was a knock at the door as an elderly priest entered.

"Mr. Hughes, may I come in?"

Robert didn't answer.

The priest took no pleasure in these situations at all. He christened Jacob and gave him God's blessing as he placed a St. Christopher pendant on his tiny body. Jacob was given the last rights, and the priest blessed Anne, who was still unconscious.

Robert cradled Jacob in his arms until his tiny heart stopped beating. A few moments later a nurse came to take his lifeless body and she had to physically unpeel Robert's fingers to remove Jacob from his hands. Robert just sat as his son was taken away.

A young mother named Jennifer had passed earlier that morning in childbirth, so the nurse asked if Jacob could be placed with her. Robert agreed. At least their son would be in the arms of a mother—a mother who would be pining for her own child.

This was the very least he could do, to try and find some comfort for their son and the young lady. Robert met her husband, who too was soul destroyed. The man stood cradling their son, wondering how the boy would cope with never knowing his mother. Robert, however, had the opposite problem, as his wife would never know their son.

The two men stood side by side as the priest recited the prayers and talked about how Jennifer and Jacob would be together on their journey back to the Lord.

Jacob was placed gently in Jennifer's arms as she lay in her coffin. Such a waste of a young woman's life, why had God called her home too?

Jennifer and Jacob were to be buried the following Friday in the church at 12 a.m., in the same church where Robert and Anne had married.

Robert took Charlotte's hand as they walked along the long cold corridor toward the hospital exit. Charlotte still hadn't uttered a single word. The stillness was almost as if the world had ended.

Anne's consultant had told Robert it would take time for Charlotte to recover, as his daughter was deeply traumatized. Robert was now carrying a huge chain of guilt, with heavy locks of steel that God had placed around his body to wear for this sin. These chains were invisible to the human eye, but not for Robert. God now held both his heart and mind, and his soul was gone from him as punishment.

Robert walked into Albert and Florence's home as Charlotte ran into her grandpapa's arms. Florence knew instantly something was wrong, even before Robert told them what had happened.

Florence almost fell to the ground with the words which were being spoken from Robert's mouth. They agreed to take Charlotte back into their home, whilst Robert tried every single day to speak to Anne, who refused to even see him. Anne was discharged home ten days later. She had not even been strong enough physically, or mentally, to go to her own son's funeral. Anne wept in her hospital bed as she thought of Jennifer, on her journey back to the Lord, who would always be cradling Anne's child, Jacob.

Robert, along with Albert, Florence, and their family, had attended the funeral of Jennifer and Jacob. The whole village had packed the church to show their respects to the two men.

Robert and David, Jennifer's husband, stood at the graveside. Their lives had been catastrophically turned upside down. They both knew their lives would never be the same again, always filled with the pain of their loss.

Florence called every day to see Anne at the hospital and occasionally called on Robert at their family home.

Albert had told Robert in no uncertain terms that he was keeping Charlotte. She had clung to her grandfather so tightly. Albert told him that his granddaughter was frightened, scared, and traumatized, and still would not speak a single word.

Once he had established what was happening with Charlotte, Albert took Robert outside and told him privately that he would like to kill him with his own bare hands.

The same went for Anne's brothers later that day, when they had heard the horrific news. However, no one in the village was told the whole truth about what had really happened that evening, all anyone knew was that Anne had had a bad fall. But at least Robert had told Albert the truth. He had owned up to it like a man, he was no coward and he would take whatever was thrown at him.

On the day of Anne's discharge, Robert went to the hospital as he had done every single day before. He had to, he would try to make amends for as long as he breathed.

Anne would be the one to decide; she could go back to the home they shared together, or she could go back to her parents. Robert hoped that one day she might be able to forgive him, and he desperately wanted her to come home.

Eventually, Anne had agreed to see him.

"I'm sorry, Anne, there are no words I could ever say, a thousand sorry, nothing could ever repair the damage I have caused."

"Words, Robert, whatever you could try and say to make this right, you have broken me. You have taken my child from my womb and my heart."

"I know, and I will live with it all my life."

Anne looked straight at him.

"I shall go back to our house with Charlotte under these conditions. You are never to drink again. You will never touch me again. To the outside world, we will be a normal family. They will just see a family in deep mourning, but inside that door, we are broken. To Charlotte in her waking hours, we will carry on in our daily duties, as I will not have her broken, and I will always protect her."

"I will agree to anything, Anne."

Her terms agreed, Anne left the hospital with Robert and went back to their family home. Florence called to check on Anne every day, bringing Charlotte so that she could see her mother and hoping that it wouldn't be long before she could bring her back into the family fold. Charlotte still wouldn't talk, even when she saw her mother. However, after two months of daily visits, Charlotte suddenly spoke and cried into her mummy's arms.

Anne brought Charlotte closer to her, leaving Robert further apart from the two of them. Robert had made an agreement with Anne, God, and Jacob, that no matter what, he would take whatever came his way, for he had caused this pain, and no one else.

Chapter 7:
Darkness

To the outside world, they were a family in mourning, but hopefully, with time they would be able to rebuild their lives. Robert worked hard at the mill, doing everything in his power to be the perfect husband and father. He knew he had broken his wife, and nothing could repair what he had done to her.

Charlotte was now seven, and the trauma that happened when she was just two years of age was not even a memory. Robert had devoted his every waking hour to her and her mother.

Anne, meanwhile, was just existing. Every day she thought of Jacob, but Charlotte was her life. Her little girl needed her, and she did everything she could for her child. This precious little girl, she would devote her life to ensuring no harm would ever come to her, and she would not allow a living soul to cause her any harm.

Anne continued her daily duties as a wife and even slept in the same bed as Robert. He never touched her body again from that day, but he was the perfect husband and father in his daily role. Robert also never went out drinking again.

One day, Robert took Charlotte for a walk through the bluebell wood. It was July, and the sun was shining brightly through the trees as he watched Charlotte playing blissfully. It took him back to the days he had walked with her mother, remembering when she was a small baby in her pram. Life had changed so much, and the wonderful walks he had shared with her mother were no longer taken together.

"Come on, Charlotte, time to get back, your mother will be cross, we will be late for dinner!"

"Really, Daddy? Please, a little longer?"

"Come on, Charlotte, I don't want to make your mummy cross with me."

Charlotte was still moaning as her father asked again. Robert and Charlotte in fact just made it home in time. Charlotte played around with her food and didn't eat much at all. Robert thought she was sulking because she had had to come home.

Anne cleared the table away and started on the washing up. Robert told Charlotte it was bath time. He loved the shifts that enabled him to spend this time with her, and which meant he could read her storybooks as she fell asleep.

Robert checked on Charlotte a couple of hours later. As he pulled the covers back over her, he noticed she was running a temperature. Suddenly Charlotte stirred.

"Daddy! Why are there lizards on my bed?"

She was now becoming delirious too.

"Anne!" he screamed, "Call for the doctor! It's Charlotte, she is sick."

Robert was frantic with worry, as fear of what could happen raced through his mind.

Anne ran as fast as she could to Dr. Sunderland's surgery, banging heavily on his door.

"Please, Doctor, come quickly, it's our Charlotte!"

The doctor grabbed his bag and ran out of the door with Anne.

They arrived at the house with great speed, and he began immediately checking Charlotte's blood pressure and her temperature. Her body was now covered in a blotchy rash, which did not fade when Dr. Sutherland rolled a glass over her skin. She complained of the light hurting her eyes as he lifted her eyelids to check her pupils. Charlotte's temperature read 39.8, and he called 999, saying she needed to go to hospital immediately.

She was indeed very sick, and he suspected meningitis. There wasn't much time, and he had to act fast to find out if it was bacterial or viral meningitis.

Robert started throwing items in a hold-all for Anne as they raced against the clock and waited for the arrival of the ambulance.

Charlotte had indeed contracted bacterial meningitis. They heard her screams as the lumbar puncture test was performed. This test was to check the fluid on her spine.

The consultant explained to Robert and Anne that Charlotte would have to stay in the hospital for around two weeks. This, though, was an approximate timescale, as the antibiotics had to be administered directly into Charlotte's veins. The consultant continued to explain that Charlotte could be left with hearing loss, maybe vision loss too. He went on to outline the many other health problems she could be left with due to meningitis, which included epilepsy, movement, and balance problems, possible loss of limbs, and that in the worst-case scenario, one in ten cases of bacterial meningitis could actually prove fatal.

Anne collapsed into Robert's arms. "Help her, Robert! Don't let her die too, please Robert, I beg of you! Why God, why? What have I done to you? Please, Robert, help her!"

This was the first time Anne had asked Robert for anything in five years.

"I will help her, Anne, I promise you I will, even if I have to sell my soul to the devil!"

Anne was now totally exhausted, both physically and mentally. Robert stayed by Charlotte's side, whilst Anne slipped into another world, completely soul-destroyed. He watched as the antibiotics entered Charlotte's veins, wondering if she would come back to them from the induced coma.

Four days passed, and it was now considered safe for the doctors to bring her out of the coma, which they had induced as a safety precaution.

Charlotte's body had needed time to fight the infection and to let the antibiotics try to kill the bacteria in her body. They would now discover if she had been left with any health issues, but she was alive, and they were at least grateful that God had not taken her along with her brother.

The test results showed that Charlotte had been left with a weakness to her limbs, possible epilepsy, some kidney problems, and hearing and sight problems too.

The doctor explained regarding epilepsy, that this could come in different forms. Time would tell if epilepsy would be an issue, although she hadn't shown any signs of it yet.

Charlotte had many hurdles to face, but Robert helped to nurse her back to health, alongside her physiotherapists and team of doctors. They also helped Anne to overcome her trauma, caused by the huge loss of Jacob, followed by the strain of Charlotte's, which had taken such a massive toll again on her body.

A team of highly trained psychologists had managed to heal the crack between Anne and Robert. Anne was eventually able to see how his persistence and total dedication to Charlotte's recovery had brought his daughter back to almost a normal life again. However, there was no doubt that the scar would always be there.

Robert taught Charlotte to walk again with the help of the doctors. With his encouragement and devotion, his daughter was slowly recovering and regaining her strength.

They had become a family again, they had learned to move forward, and time had helped them to heal. If they had lost Charlotte, they too would have died, their hearts would have completely broken, leaving them in total darkness and despair.

*****

It was on a beautiful September morning when the cry came from Anne and Robert's bedroom. God had gifted them another child, they had been given a son.

Their child came into their world weighing nine lbs., two ounces. His body was covered in dark hair and he had a huge amount of thick black hair on his head. His parents called him Luke. Charlotte laughed at her baby brother when she saw him, commenting that he looked like a monkey without a tail, at which both Anne and Robert burst into laughter.

Charlotte would be ten in December and was almost a carbon copy of her mother at that age, with her adventurous ways. Charlotte's health had its ups and downs as she was still a very weak child, although she thrived on life like any normal child of her age.

Robert called into the church later that day. He knelt down in front of the crucifix above the altar. Jacob would never be gone from their lives, but Robert wanted to thank God for his forgiveness and his gift of Luke.

Robert looked up to God as his eyes focused on God's own son, Jesus, who was persecuted, crucified on a cross, and returned to his heavenly Father's arms. Robert spoke aloud and promised that he would always prove himself to God and adhere to his Ten Commandments and to the word of God. Robert then spoke of his promise to always protect his family, and he sought forgiveness for what he had done when his son lost his life.

Robert then asked the Lord to keep Jacob close in his arms, until the day he called him home too. When that day came, Robert would take his son Jacob back into his own arms. He arose from the altar and thanked God again for the gift of Luke.

Chapter 8:
The Coming of Age

The years had flown by, and Charlotte was now a grown woman of almost 21. Robert and Anne had been busy organizing a party for her, much to her little brother's annoyance. Luke desperately wanted to go to the party, but his parents said no, he was too young, and it was Charlotte's party, not his. Luke wasn't going to give up, he knew what he had to do.

"Charlotte, please can I come, please, Charlotte? You know how I always like to watch you dance! And tonight, you will be wearing mother's red shoes, and you always used to let me play in them too, because you didn't want to get caught wearing them! I promise, Charlotte, I will let you wear them all night tonight, and I won't tell on you!" he teased her.

Charlotte adored her little brother. Although her mother and father's love were so immense for her, Luke was different, he gave her parents something different to focus on.

Her parents never pushed her out, and she was always included. They were so tight as a family and extremely protective of each other. Charlotte's family now lived life very cautiously, though, avoiding anything that could involve any form of danger.

One time, Luke had been invited to go camping with his school friend Matthew, but his parents had said in a polite and kind manner, that he couldn't because of the danger he might get into.

Anne suggested instead that the boys camped out in their garden one weekend, to Luke's great delight. He enjoyed the experience of camping out under the stars with the protection of his parents close by.

Charlotte and Luke understood the fears their parents held in their hearts. They both knew they had had a brother who had died just after he was born. Her parents never told them how they just said that life was a precious gift, and they must be careful not to live it in vain for Jacob's sake.

Charlotte had had many things happen to her at school, and Luke, who was aware of what she was going through, was told sharply by Charlotte never to utter a word to their parents. Luke knew that when Charlotte spoke sharply to him like that, she really meant it. However, Luke had never known the intensity of what she went through, or the secrets that Charlotte was hiding inside her.

"Luke, OK, you can come to the party!"

"Yippee!"

Luke then ran off to get ready.

Charlotte knew her party wouldn't be the same without Luke, but her parents had wanted her to be able to choose if her little brother was to come or not. Now 21 old, she was getting the key to the door, and she would be officially classed as an adult. Charlotte could now vote, she could marry, and could drive—the world was hers for the taking.

How her life was so very different from her mother's! Her mother had been married twice by 21, had had a child, and had even lost one by that age.

Charlotte's party was being held in the village hall, complete with a live band. She was a young girl who had been given the best of everything, as well as love, and her party was going to be no exception.

Charlotte's party had been the talk of the village. Some may have thought she was spoiled, but most of them saw a girl who deserved the world. Robert and Anne had given her everything she ever wanted, and Charlotte showed her gratitude in her manners and was never spiteful or cruel. As a family, though, they never traveled, feeling that life in the village was all that they needed.

Robert and Anne wanted her to have the best coming of age party and had saved hard for this special day. Her father had worked hard, and her mother had even taken a job in the village shop. Anne loved her little job, it got her out and helped with her recovery, causing no distress to the children as they were at school. Anne's hours fitted in with the family, and Robert didn't mind, as he didn't want Anne at home having time to think about Jacob. Little did he know that every day Anne thought of her baby, her Jacob and his journey with Jennifer.

"Charlotte!" Robert was calling her.

"Yes, I'm in my room."

Robert came in with two boxes, a large box, and a small one. Anne was behind him, with Luke running up the stairs like a Tasmanian devil, not wanting to miss anything.

"Charlotte, here's your birthday gift, we love you so much!"

Charlotte opened the small box with apprehension, finding inside a beautiful gold watch awaiting her delicate wrist.

"Thank you so much, Mum, thank you, Dad."

"What about me?" Luke said.

"And of course, we love you too, Luke," laughter filling the room.

Charlotte began to open her second box. It was so neatly presented with a green and black ribbon magnificently wrapped around the box to hold it together. Harrods of London logo in fine gold ink, telling the world this was from a store of excellence.

The box promised a gift that epitomized class. Anne knew how much Charlotte had adored the store since she was a small child when her father had treated Charlotte and her mother on a trip to London. This was only one of a few times they had left the village, as Anne used the village as a place of sanctuary.

Charlotte was unaware that the date of their trip had been the anniversary date of when Jacob had passed. Robert had wanted to give Anne some form of solace and peace for her thoughts, as he knew this day was always a dark one for her, so he had organized a trip to the store as a treat. As for Robert, he continued to carry the chains of guilt and sorrow around his body, weighed down with heavy locks of steel.

That trip had been Charlotte's first encounter with Harrods, and she remembered how impressed she had been as a child with this huge store. A store filled with everything from toys, sweets, and clothes—a place of pure indulgence! These huge windows had been spectacular, cascading beauty and opulence as Charlotte gasped.

Charlotte hadn't even opened the box fully yet, she was so enthralled by it. Charlotte often spent many hours going through magazines, as she had a complete fascination with fashion. Charlotte lifted the lid off the white box, carefully placing the green and black ribbon to one side. She admired the beautiful light tissue paper, neatly hiding the surprise inside. Charlotte slowly unpeeled the tissue paper, trying to savor every moment. Beautiful red material shone back at her.

"Wow!" she exclaimed, as she lifted out the material.

A dress more beautiful than any she had ever seen in her magazines was sparkling brightly as she held it up against her body. It was a tea-length design, with a full-bodied skirt and red netting underneath, and a boat neckline. Three-quarter sleeves finished the impressive design.

Charlotte kissed her parents and Luke.

"Urgh, Sissy, that's disgusting!" he said as he wiped his face, "now I have to wash again!"

Charlotte laughed. Anne went to her bedroom; a stunning dress she had chosen for herself lay on her bed.

Once she was dressed, Anne sprayed herself with Opium perfume and admired the way the French navy dress clung to her beautiful frame. The heavy material showed the elegance of the cut and its simplicity.

The party would be starting soon. Anne's parents, alongside her brothers and their wives, would be there.

Charlotte's cousins had had many conversations about it between themselves—they too were excited and had enjoyed planning their own outfits. Anne and Robert's family were now so huge that two hundred people would pack the village hall.

Anne was adding the final touches to her makeup, and she beamed with pride as she saw Charlotte in the reflection of her mirror, dressed in her new red dress and her mother's beautiful red shoes.

"Charlotte, you look stunning, my beautiful daughter!"

Anne's eyes filled with tears. Charlotte was unaware that her mother had been wearing a red dress and those very same red shoes the night she had fainted and found out that she was carrying Charlotte. Up till now, John seldom made many entrances to Anne's mind; for to her, Dr. John Andrews had died long ago.

As for Robert, he had blanked John's name from his mind. John Andrews was a bastard, a coward, and a lowlife, and didn't deserve to be a father or even know Charlotte's beauty. Robert also knew he wasn't much better than him regarding being a husband to Anne, because of his part in what had happened to Jacob.

Although Luke had come along, Robert still carried that ghost on his back.

Robert didn't know either that Anne had been wearing a red dress and those red shoes on that fateful night when she found out she was pregnant with Charlotte.

Robert had only been informed by Anne that Charlotte had wanted a red dress for her birthday party, as she was planning to wear her mother's special red shoes, which she had always admired.

Anne thought of John too at that moment, and how much her world had changed since he had given her those red shoes. A world she had thought was hers, a magical and dreamy place for her to dance in with her love. This life she was living now was so completely different from the one she had imagined with John.

Fortunately, Anne had managed to piece her heart together and rebuild her life.

Her eyes fixated back on Charlotte, her innocent and beautiful girl. Charlotte would not be standing there if she had listened to John, yet Charlotte wasn't even aware of his existence. She was Anne's child, and John had made his decision when he abandoned her in that room and didn't come back, agreement or not. John had made his choice. Anne was confident that days like this belonged completely and solely to her.

"Mother! It's just liked the Audrey Hepburn dress in the magazine! And thank you for all the years you let me play in your precious red shoes. I can finally now wear them, without worrying about getting into trouble! I will treasure them forever. I shall pass them over to my little girl when I have one!" she giggled.

Anne checked Charlotte over, she looked amazing. Robert's face, when he saw his daughter, was a picture in itself. Robert became emotional, taking a hankie from his pocket as he told Anne and Luke, "Right, time to take our Charlotte to her party!" in a proud fatherly tone.

Everyone was already there awaiting Charlotte, as Robert and Anne opened the village hall door. Everyone then started to sing Happy Birthday to Charlotte, followed by several Hip-Hip-Hoorays!

Charlotte's best friend from school, Dawn, was there with her boyfriend Andy, along with Robert's boss and work colleagues. Charlotte mingled amongst her guests, being a perfect hostess with impeccable manners.

Charlotte noticed that Dawn and Andy were talking to a most attractive man, who was that? Her mind puzzled.

Charlotte blushed and her mother caught sight of her. Anne recognized that look.

The expression on her daughter's face took her back again, back to when she had first met John. John, who was father to this beautiful girl, this beautiful girl who practically didn't exist in his mind. 21 years, and nothing to show of their relationship apart from the court hearing in London, when the judge had ordered him to pay an amount every month toward Charlotte's upkeep. How he had tried so hard to not pay, offering so many excuses, pleading with the judge that she was not his responsibility.

Robert had told John after the hearing, "Don't worry about it, Dr. Andrews, you keep your money! I'm Charlotte's father, and I will be so all her life."

Robert had always classed Charlotte as his own, and he never wanted any of John's money.

"John Andrews, God created a monster instead of a man. To never know the love of that beautiful child! You have thrown away the most precious gift from God. I will always be her father, and I always have been."

Robert could not suppress his frustration and anger at the man.

Anne approached Charlotte, who still seemed to be blushing.

"Charlotte, Granny Florence was wondering if you could spare her a few moments?"

Anne's eye was always watching over her daughter, but she was also trying hard not to be an overbearing and overprotective mother.

"Yes, of course, Mother." But Charlotte was still wondering, *who was that handsome man who had made her blush?*

The night soon came to a close, but what a wonderful evening she had had! She was now a young lady with the world at her feet. She had big plans for her future, but she didn't know how to approach her parents about what she wanted to do. She knew how protective they were, but the tiny village and her job in the office at the local mill was no longer enough for Charlotte, she wanted more. She loved fashion, she wanted to see the world, she was driven and knew she had to do what was right for her.

Charlotte had been heading girl, an outstanding student at school, although at times she had suffered at the hands of some nasty bullies. Her parents never knew about them, as she had held that part deep and close inside. Luke had known, as he had witnessed some of it as they walked home from school. The girls were quite jealous of Charlotte, maybe because her mother always made sure that Charlotte had the best in clothes. This seemed to cause a lot of jealousy at school, but Charlotte hid it well.

Luke was told by Charlotte never to tell anyone about the bullying, as she thought it would cause even more trouble for her.

When she came home one day with some cuts and bruises, she told her parents that she had had a rough time at netball and had fallen. Her mother had taken it quite seriously and had arranged for Charlotte to have some tests, fearing that the fall might be related to what had happened when she was small and had had meningitis. They tested her for epilepsy, but all the results came back negative. They said she would outgrow the falls, as they were part of her changing into a lady from a child. Little did her mother and father know the truth.

Chapter 9:
Changes

"Mum, I need to talk to you and Dad."

"Is everything OK, Charlotte darling, are you feeling well?" Her mother always feared for Charlotte's health.

"Yes, Mum." Charlotte drew a big breath, "Mum, I want to leave the village, I want to go to London, I want to work in the city, please, Mum, can I?"

Anne's face must have spoken the words without uttering a single word, so Robert stepped in,

"Charlotte, what has brought this on, aren't you happy working in the mill? I think Mr. Griffins would have a heart attack if you left the mill, you run that office, what would he do without you?"

"Please, Dad, please!"

He looked at Anne.

"But you don't have a job, Charlotte, you know no one, and a city can be a dangerous place!"

"Mum, Dad, I know, but you have brought me up to live life, to work hard, and to live my dreams. This is my dream; I have wanted it for ages!"

Charlotte then showed them all the applications she had filled out and never posted.

"Well, Charlotte, if this is what you want, then you must do it. But not until you get the right position, have sorted the right accommodation and we know the full aspects. If this is all in order, then we have no choice but to let you go and try."

"Oh, Mum, Dad, thank you, thank you!"

Charlotte soon got her job and accommodation sorted, and despite her parents' own personal heartache, they kept their side of the agreement.

Charlotte left the village, and they waved her off from the station. Charlotte had a week to settle into her apartment before she started work in a large fashion house. She was given a subsidy from her employers toward her accommodation as she was working in the inner-city belt.

Charlotte was nervous on her first day but was soon put at her ease by the office girls and some of the young men— although she was unaware that these young men were trying to get her attention. Despite being naive, she was grown up in other ways, and she thrived in the workplace.

Two months had passed, and Charlotte loved nothing more than kicking off her shoes at lunchtime to relax in Hyde Park. She had her favorite spot, and every day took herself off and sat in the striped green or blue deck chairs by the bandstand. Sometimes she found herself dreaming away as she watched the sky, the clouds moving, making different shapes as the seconds passed. Some afternoons, Charlotte was almost late due to her daydreaming.

As spring turned into summer, autumn, and then winter, so many changes had happened.

Charlotte watched the colors of the seasons change in her beloved park, Hyde Park. She had seen the laughter and fun that the park generated with its ever-evolving circles of daily activities which were as regular as clockwork. She watched the business bankers rushing their sandwiches down on the go, whizzing through the park. They never seemed to have any time. Charlotte often thought she would love to run and almost trip in front of them to stop them for just a few minutes. Just to try and slow down their pace, as the pace was already so fast in the city.

Change was happening everywhere. London was changing; it was after all now the 1980s. The mobile phone had been the latest phenomenon to hit. *Why did so many people carry this brick thing to their ear...?* Charlotte thought.

She had grown to love it all so much, the music, the musicals, the city, and its lights. The speed of the city, the smell of the awful tube, the roads—it was a city of complete craziness, a complete rat race. London was basically busy people rushing everywhere, but she loved it, actually, she absolutely adored the power of the city.

It was a far cry from the tiny Yorkshire village her mother, father and Luke still lived in. They often checked on her and had even made a few trips to London to see her.

She was looking forward to going back to Yorkshire at Christmas. It was magical, with its beautiful winter scenery, and always drew her back. Charlotte adored London, but the empowering love of her family always made her want to go back to the warmth and tenderness of her family at Christmas.

She had saved well, she had compiled a magnificent Christmas list, and she couldn't wait to see everyone. Her mother was absolutely fascinated by Harrods and Charlotte had brought the most overindulgent hamper.

She couldn't wait to take it home to her parents, along with the amazing Christmas treasures she had found on her many shopping trips. It was going to be the most magical Christmas that Yorkshire had ever seen.

Charlotte had planned it all in her mind. She wanted to show her parents how much she appreciated the fact that all of her life they had worked hard for her to have everything, and the same with her brother Luke. They had devoted themselves completely to their children.

Now Charlotte's biggest worry was how on earth was she going to carry everything! Umm, many a conversation went over and over in Charlotte's mind.

Charlotte's last day at work arrived, and she had a schedule that Ebenezer Scrooge would have seen fit to bestow on his dedicated Marley. She had so much to do.

She had her last items to pick up from Harrods directly after work. She was due her last pay packet for December today, and this one would include her bonus. She had no idea how much to expect. The company demanded the best from its employees all year round and looked for total dedication to their jobs.

Charlotte's first bonus was exciting. Charlotte had already budgeted well to allow for her special Christmas treats for her family. She had only allocated her wage but depending on her bonus she had seen the most beautiful cardigan that would go with the red shoes that her mother had given to her for her birthday! She had adored these shoes since she was a child, and for some reason, she felt that they played a huge part in her life, but she didn't know why. One thing she was certain of though; this cardigan would go with her shoes like a glove to a lady's hand.

"Charlotte! Charlotte!" Penny was screeching across the office floor, "Open your wage packet!"

They were both at the same level, so she knew by Penny's screeching that they had received a good bonus.

In addition to that, in the last year, the fashion house had attracted many more designers, and the New York fashion show had been a complete sell-out. The whole department knew they could be in line for a great bonus, but Charlotte always played life cautiously.

"OK, Penny, I'm coming!" almost spilling her hot soup, as she headed toward her desk.

Charlotte had been awarded over seven thousand pounds. She almost fainted when she saw the figure staring back at her. Charlotte's father's annual salary was just double that while working as a manager of a mill back in Yorkshire. How different life and money were in the big city!

"Wow, Penny, I am definitely going to Harrods after work, are you going to Harrods?"

"Yes, Charlotte, can we please go to the food hall? They have the most beautiful Christmas tarts. I want to take some home for my mother!"

"Of course, Penny, we will indeed!"

Charlotte needed no excuse to visit her beloved Harrods, especially at Christmas. The office was buzzing for the rest of the afternoon, so not much work was actually done. The office was shutting down for the Christmas festivities, and they were all looking forward to seeing their loved ones. It was now the 23rd December, tomorrow would be Christmas Eve, and soon she would be back home in her Yorkshire village. Charlotte's parents and Luke were eagerly awaiting her arrival.

"Charlotte, come on, it is going to be crazy in there tonight!"

"OK, Penny, I'm coming! I just need to do my hat, my gloves, and my lipstick!"

"Wow! Charlotte, you look like one of those mannequins in the windows of Harrods!"

"Oh, shut up, Penny, you're being ridiculous!" she laughed.

"Where the hell did you get that coat and hat from?"

"Well, one of the girls who did the shoot for the fashion show was given as a sample, but she didn't like the color! So, I asked the boss if I could have it, and I added some extra touches and made it my own."

"Charlotte, you look like you belong to a wealthy family, you don't even look like you work for a living!"

"Penny, your imagination does run wild at times, you really do make me laugh!"

Penny and Charlotte arrived outside Harrods, marveling at the spectacular lights wrapped around the magnificent store. Huge windows displayed the current fashions, which were arranged with flair and creativity to tempt you into the temple of magnificent indulgence for the rich and famous. A temple where the money had no meaning—a stark contrast to the other part of society which realistically had to save very hard for a special item. It was also a beautiful place for people who perhaps simply wanted to buy one delicious chocolate, or to walk around the department store to breathe in the magic that the store expelled.

Charlotte agreed with Penny that they would split up and purchase their gifts, and they arranged to meet at the Brampton Road exit in two hours' time.

Charlotte arrived at the floor of Women's Wear, totally unaware that she looked like a supermodel herself. She was also unaware of the attention she was drawing, even though Penny had constantly told her how stunning she was. She did not realize that the throw-out sample she was wearing was actually in one of Harrods shop windows.

In fact, the coat was so in demand that it had become number one on the wish list of the Harrods ladies this Christmas. Some of the customers who noticed Charlotte assumed that Harrods had hired a model to walk the floors, to generate orders of the designer coat.

Charlotte's beauty was just like her mother's, and both of them were unaware of the effect they had on others. Charlotte actually didn't realize that people had begun to follow her.

She finally found the cardigan. This would be the most expensive item she had ever brought. It was a classic like her mother's red shoes and she would have it forever.

Her parents would have a fit if they knew how much she had paid for it, Charlotte thought, remembering the hours she had seen her father work over the years.

The sales assistant finished wrapping the garment and handed it to Charlotte, when for the first time in her life, Charlotte was hit with a powerful memory. She remembered she was holding her precious bunny rabbit, waiting for her daddy to come home.

She remembered her mother telling her he was working late.

She then recalled her mummy at the top of the stairs. All of a sudden Charlotte hit the floor.

"Hello, are you OK?" The man looking down at her had eyes as blue as the sky. Charlotte stared at him in confusion. This was the handsome man she had seen talking to Dawn and Andy at her party.

Charlotte was really dazed as she started to speak. "I am terribly sorry, I must have fainted!"

Charlotte tried to stand as she saw people all around her.

These were not the faces of anyone she knew, and she felt faint again.

"Miss Charlotte?"

It was the blue-eyed man again. He explained that his name was Charles. Charles spoke with a strong firm voice.

"Harry, please fetch the lift chair, we will take Miss Charlotte to my office immediately." Charles was calling for the First Aid officer. Charlotte was still dazed and totally oblivious to her surroundings, she had no idea what was actually going on around her at that point.

"Please bring Miss Charlotte's purchases to my office, Natalie."

Charlotte came around to find herself surrounded by the splendor and richness of dark oak furniture, amid the opulence of someone's extremely grand office.

"Miss Charlotte, you seem to have fainted and banged your head as you hit the floor."

"I don't recall what happened. I felt hot whilst in the department store… I was paying for my cardigan."

"Well, Miss Charlotte, you seemed to have drawn quite a lot of attention to yourself by that stage!"

"Really?"

"It seems that apart from Harrods, you are the only other person in possession of our window display coat."

"I am?" asked Charlotte, looking even more puzzled. It was Charles's job to know anything and everything that was happening in Harrods.

"So, either you are the designer, which of course I know you are not…"

"Sir, I haven't done anything wrong, it's mine, this is a sample from the fashion house!"

Charles laughed at her, "Charlotte, still so very innocent! I can still remember your face when you entered the village hall on the night of your party!"

Charlotte was now looking completely startled.

"How do you know Dawn and Andy? And how did you come to be at my party?"

"I was visiting Andrew who worked in the Mill in Yorkshire, looking at the quality of the wool, for a particular garment that we were working on. Harrods prides itself on selling only the finest to our clientele, so we are directly involved even before the production line stage."

Charles explained how Andrew had been pushed for time because of a special party that was happening that evening, and he had asked Charles along to meet some of the mill workers who helped produce the tweed.

"I see, I am so sorry, it's been rather an eventful day!"

"That's OK, Miss Charlotte."

"Oh, no, my friend Penny! I am supposed to meet her, she will be waiting at the Brampton Road exit!"

"Do not worry, I will send a call to have her brought up. And please may I offer the Harrods courtesy car to take you home?"

Charlotte and Penny were delighted with the offer of the chauffeur.

"Charlotte, I look forward to seeing you at Andrew and Dawn's wedding after the festivities—they told me that we would both be invited when I saw them at your party."

Charlotte smiled politely and they said their goodbyes. With that they left the office, closing the door behind them.

"Have you gone absolutely flaming mad, Charlotte? Did you see how handsome he was?"

"Penny, please, I just want to go home."

"What happened anyway, Charlotte?"

"I'm sorry, I don't want to sound mean, Penny, I just want to go home now."

"I wish we had a camera with us to take a picture of us in the Harrods car!"

"Oh, Penny, only you!"

Charlotte was glad to get into her apartment, and she asked the driver to pass on her thanks to Charles for his kind gesture. Penny immediately began ordering a pizza delivery at the same time as giving orders for Charlotte to have a hot bath. The plan was that after that, they could chill and relax on the sofa.

Charles had given a note to the driver with strict instructions on it to see Charlotte safely home, and the driver passed this on to Penny. The note had Charles's telephone number written on it in case of an emergency.

Charlotte was soaking in the bath, as her mind began taking her back to the moment of Mr. Rabbit again. She suddenly bolted upright in the bath. *What the hell is wrong with me, my mind is on overdrive!* she thought, just as she heard the doorbell ring through the apartment.

Penny then began screeching to say that dinner was ready.

Charlotte awoke in the morning feeling refreshed as she thought of yesterday's events. It must have been over-excitement, and the rush of last-minute shopping, that had made her feel strange. The wonderful bonus she had received as well as the heat in Harrods, that must have been why she fainted. This was what she was trying to convince herself, although she couldn't help wondering why she was having these thoughts involving Mr. Rabbit.

Charlotte had learned a strong form of mind power, which she had taught herself to do when bad things happened at school. She had taught herself to keep worrying thoughts locked away. These were haunting ghosts that would sometimes appear, giving her terrible nightmares and flashbacks. Never did Charlotte's parents know of her terrible secrets. So why now were these feelings resurfacing with the appearance of Mr. Rabbit?

Charlotte slept most of her journey back to Yorkshire on the train. Butterflies fluttered in her stomach with anticipation, as her train pulled into her station. Her father would be waiting for her with Luke, and her mother would be busy cooking and preparing ahead for the Christmas festivities.

The train roared into the station, the guard blowing hard on his whistle to announce their arrival. Charlotte drew down the window of the carriage door, as the guard began to help Charlotte from the train. She passed the hamper to the guard as she took hold of her case. He looked quite starstruck as if he had just helped a famous movie star off the train. People began to clear from the platform, but she still could not see her father or Luke.

"Where are they?"

Just then a break appeared amongst the crowd, and she could finally see her father and Luke, who were searching frantically for her too.

"Dad, Luke, I'm here!"

As for their response, they just stared at her. They weren't sure, was that really their Charlotte?

"Daddy, Luke, it's me!"

"Sissy, bloody hell, Sissy, I didn't recognize you!"

"Luke!" his father responded sharply. "I have told you before my lad, about using that mill talk!"

"Well, well, what do we have here then?" Charlotte started to giggle, her excitement getting the better of her.

"Charlotte, what a fine young lady you have grown into, too fine for these Yorkshire Dales I would say!"

"Oh, Dad, don't be daft, you can't take the Yorkshire out of the girl you know!" Charlotte would never lose her roots or forget where she came from.

"I am just a lady of substance!" she burst out laughing.

"Come on, you two, Mother will be cross if we are late!"

The journey wasn't long from the station, around ten minutes. Robert knew Anne would be clock watching, waiting for her daughter to get home.

"Charlotte, finally you're home!"

That was the first moment in Anne's life when she fully understood how her own parents must have felt when she had left the village and returned to see them.

"Look at our beautiful daughter, happy birthday darling!"

This was the first year Charlotte had not been at home for her birthday. And now she was 22 years old, where had that year gone?

"What has London done to our girl? Is that really you Charlotte?"

"Oh, Mother!" she laughed, "Come and look at what I have brought you!"

"Oh, my goodness, Charlotte!" Her mother was almost lost for words when she opened the magnificent hamper.

"Robert, come quickly!" Her father was wondering what possibly could be exciting about a hamper.

"Look at what Charlotte has brought us from Harrods! Only the finest jams, biscuits, teas, fruit cake, and chocolates!"

Anne found it impossible to contain her excitement, as she thanked her daughter again.

"Robert!"

"Yes, Anne, I can see, it's not for me, though—all that rich proper stuff."

Charlotte suddenly felt there was a tone of resentment in her father's voice but could not understand why.

"Well, Robert, we shall see when the bread comes out of the oven, let's see you resist then!"

Robert must have realized what he had said.

"Charlotte, I didn't mean to sound ungrateful. I've just never had this fancy stuff before."

"It's OK, Dad, honestly!"

Christmas was just as Charlotte had imagined it to be, simply wonderful.

Chapter 10:
Love and the Darkest Day

"Charlotte, Charlotte!"

Dawn called out for her, "Please, could you help my mother with arranging my veil, I think she is about to cry all over it!"

"Yes, of course, Dawn!"

"Mrs. Myers, would you like some help?"

"Thank you, Charlotte darling, I am feeling a little overwhelmed!"

"Oh, Dawn, you look amazing!"

A beautiful white lace gown clung to Dawn's frame, as her mother passed the veil to Charlotte. Her veil was so delicate, with such intricate detail, and it complimented her stunning gown perfectly.

The lace had been commissioned from the finest lace makers in Nottingham, and the designer had spent many hours perfecting the gown with Mrs. Myers and Dawn.

The design they had chosen was so intricate that it needed the best lace-makers around to bring this gown to life. Dawn was Mr. and Mrs. Myer's only child, and Mrs. Myers wanted her daughter to have the wedding of her dreams, no matter the cost. Dawn had chosen to wear fresh flowers as her headpiece, and she made a beautiful bride.

Charlotte wore her special red shoes, along with a red gown which had a magnificent cape to compliment it.

Dawn had chosen the cape for Charlotte especially, for she knew that her December wedding might be extremely cold, and she couldn't have Charlotte falling ill.

Dawn knew all about Charlotte and the health issues she had faced as a child because they had grown up together. Dawn had three other bridesmaids who would be dressed identically to Charlotte, so Dawn simply explained that she wanted them all to wear capes as part of her Christmas theme. Charlotte never found out her friend's real reason.

Dawn also decided to wear a cape, a gorgeous white fur-lined one. However, she had decided she would only wear it after the wedding service, not before, cold or not. She wanted to wear a traditional veil for the first part of the ceremony when she would exchange her vows with Andy.

Dawn, along with her parents and the main wedding party arrived five minutes early, and the priest was awaiting them eagerly outside the Catholic Church.

Dawn's mother walked down the aisle so gracefully, Andy was beaming with pride as he smiled at his future mother-in-law. He now knew that Dawn was here and that this is where they would soon become husband and wife, here in God's house.

The organist began playing as Dawn made her entrance, her father proudly holding his daughter's arm, as he led her down the aisle to her beloved Andy.

Charlotte and the three bridesmaids followed with ease and grace, supporting Dawn as they walked closely behind her.

The church pews were filled with family and friends, and the cascading essence of frankincense and myrrh fille d every inch of the church.

The day passed so quickly—the exchanging of the rings, the speeches, the cutting of the cake and Dawn and Andy's first dance.

"Now, let's get the party started!"

The bridesmaids were eager to show off their dancing skills, as the DJ played a mix up of music from the decades. The dance floor came alive as the rest of the guests took to the dance floor, and the room filled with laughter and magic.

"Hello, Charlotte!"

She had forgotten that Charles would be there!

"How are you feeling now?"

"Much better, thank you, Charles!"

"Charlotte, you look absolutely beautiful!"

Charlotte felt her cheeks blushing almost the same color as her gown.

"That's very kind of you to say, Charles."

"Would it be too forward of me, Charlotte, to ask if I may have the next dance with you?"

Charlotte and Charles talked and danced most of the night away. That was the beginning of their own journey together, her red shoes taking her toward a new path of love.

From that day on, with the exception of a week apart, they never spent a single day away from each other, and within nine months they had moved in together. Robert and Anne soon became very fond of Charles, for they could see his complete dedication and love toward Charlotte.

Charles had introduced Charlotte to all the finest restaurants in London, and she had learned so much from him over the past nine months. He was Charlotte's destiny, and she felt sure that she had found her soulmate and trusted companion. They would walk the same path together on their journey through life, guiding and helping each other. Charlotte thought of fate, and how their paths had crossed, and she was convinced that you didn't mess with either fate or God's way.

They simply adored each other. Charles was such a distinguished man, with a wonderful character, and endearing mannerisms. His gentle persona along with his` kindness had a calming effect on anyone in his presence.

His only fault seemed to be that Charles had a very dry personality, which meant some people were not quite sure of him at times. *He could be a little too dry*, Charlotte thought to herself on a few occasions.

Charlotte and Charles were married quietly on the 13th of February 1998. Sadly, none of their parents attended the service; just four friends. Tragedy had overtaken their lives.

******

Charlotte had fallen pregnant, but she had miscarried their child at 19 weeks. Their lives had been turned upside down. They had lost their child, the only child they would ever have together. She was their little girl, a beautiful precious girl made from love from two people, although made out of wedlock and classed as a sin in God's teachings. They named her Courtney. She had been taken away from them back to God.

Charlotte had had to undergo a full hysterectomy and had her ovaries removed, immediately after losing their child. They also took the lining of her stomach away.

Charlotte at this time was still only 25 years old.

"Why, Charles? Why?"

"I don't know, Charlotte, I don't know."

Charlotte sank into a deep depression whilst in hospital. She had cried as they prepared her for theatre, knowing that her womb was to be removed and that she would never carry a child again from that day. Charles was holding her tightly, as she wept into his arms. They would never forget the date of 17th October 1994.

Anne appeared just before she went into theatre.

"My darling, my poor darling!"

Anne helped Charlotte and Charles through their journey to the operating theatre, and she stayed at the hospital helping Charles and Charlotte. She needed to be with her daughter but was trying not to overshadow Charles, as she knew his heart had also been broken. And he was grieving too. *How different he was from John*, she thought, *how so very different from John!*

Anne left around a week later to go back to Robert and their home. She knew this was going to be a long painful journey back to Yorkshire. She told Charlotte that Luke was going to come and stay with her, to help look after her, as soon as he could. Her father had also wished he could have been with her, but he knew that it was her mother she had needed at this time.

The National Express coach set on its journey, taking Anne back to her Yorkshire home.

"Why, God? Why are you still punishing me, why are you punishing Charlotte?"

Anne sobbed quietly for most of the journey home, and later, she herself sank once again into a deep depression. Her heart began aching, as every scar that had been stitched over with time opened. Each stitch that opened as painful as the one before. Anne could feel the blood pouring from her broken heart.

Charlotte stayed in the hospital for 16 days and Charles and his parents visited her every day. Charlotte had contracted a urine infection from the catheter that had been fitted after the operation. Her was body was weak, but with time it would heal.

A month had passed since Charlotte had lost her child and her womb. It was now the 19th of November 1994, and she was resting on the sofa when she heard a knock at their door. Charlotte heard Charles call out to her that Luke had arrived, Luke was here.

"It will be OK, Sissy. It will be OK."

Charles made Luke a cup of tea, then he went back to the kitchen so the two of them could have some time alone. Later, Charles was preparing a joint of lamb as Luke walked into the kitchen.

"Can I help, Charles?"

Luke noticed that Charles's eyes were filled with tears.

He wasn't a man that would normally cry, but he was so grateful that Luke had arrived. Charlotte needed her brother there with her, and these were tears of relief.

As Charles turned to get a tissue to wipe his eyes, he noticed the cat tucking into the lamb joint he had been preparing for dinner. Charles was totally horrified, but as he threw the meat into the bin, Luke almost had a fit.

"What are you doing Charles? You can't waste it, just wash it!"

How Charles's and Luke's worlds were so different!

"I know, why don't we go out for dinner?" Luke asked Charlotte. "You need to get out, Sissy!"

"I'm fine, Luke, I really don't want to. It's cold and I would rather stay in. Luke, I'm sorry." She looked across at Charles for support.

Luke could tell that she wasn't fine at all, as they were very close. He had always been grateful that Charlotte still protected him in anything he did, as he protected her, holding her secrets in. Now that she needed him, she was his Sissy, he didn't know what to do. How could he fix her? How could he help? Luke felt like he needed some space, he needed to find a solution.

"OK, Sissy, I think I might pop out and see my mate Michael for a bit then. I won't be late, love you, Sissy!" With a tear in his eye, he left the room, his heart aching at seeing his sister in pain. Charles walked with him to the door, and he saw the tears in Luke's eyes.

"It's OK, Luke," That was all that Charles said.

"See you later, Charles."

Charlotte had cared for him his whole life, and she had always loved him deeply. Luke, in turn, had always been happy to do anything for her. Charlotte had even made him dress as a girl, as a small child! She would experiment on him with the perfume she had made from roses, trying hairstyles on him too, and still Luke never complained.

Charles walked into the lounge. Charlotte had drifted off to sleep again, so Charles decided he would take this time to catch up on work. He headed toward his study, which was situated next to the lounge. Charles often spent many hours these days with his own thoughts, trying to come to terms with their loss.

Almost three hours had passed before Charles noticed the time on the clock. Charlotte was still sleeping on the sofa.

"Charlotte?"

She began to stir as she opened her eyes to the sound of his voice, still half asleep.

"Charles, can we go to bed, please? I am still feeling extremely tired. I just feel so drained. Can we, Charles?" They both hardly ate these days. Neither of them had much of an appetite, they were grieving so deeply inside.

Luke had a spare key so they knew he could let himself in.

Charles was wide awake when he looked at the clock on his bedside table and saw that it was 5.46 a.m. He had been an early riser since he was a small child. Charles began tying the belt of his dressing-gown, as he looked across to Charlotte, noticing that she was still fast asleep. He quietly closed the bedroom door and headed downstairs to the kitchen.

Charles heard the sound of the letterbox as the newspaper was being pushed through. With his mug of tea in one hand, he picked the newspaper up from the mat and headed toward his study. His eyes were drawn to the light flashing on his answer machine.

"That's strange, I never heard the phone ring!"

He then remembered that he had turned the phone onto silent so that Charlotte could rest with no outside distractions. Charles pressed the play button to hear the message. It was Anne. He couldn't accept what he had just heard so he replayed it. He was not fully awake yet, surely, he must have misunderstood what Anne had said? Still struggling to absorb the message, Charles made his way to their bedroom, where Charlotte lay asleep. He was a man carrying a weight heavier than any man should be given to carry. Charles approached Charlotte's bedside and knelt by her side.

"Charlotte," he was gently trying to wake her.

"Charlotte, wake up, darling."

She slowly stirred and rolled over toward him.

"Charlotte, darling."

"Ummm… Charles?"

"Yes, darling, it's Charles." His heart was pounding so fast.

"Yes, Charles?"

"Charlotte, I need you to get up, darling. We need to go to the hospital."

"Hospital, Charles? Why, I'm fine, honest!"

"Charlotte, it's Luke, he has been in an accident. Darling, we need to go now!"

"What?" she suddenly cried out, "Luke!"

"Your mother and father are at the hospital with him now, darling, they traveled down through the night."

Charlotte was just staring at Charles.

"Luke is alive, but he is paralyzed from the neck down."

Charlotte was in a complete trance now.

"Come on, Charlotte, we need to get ready and get there as soon as possible!"

Charlotte pulled the covers from her, placing her feet on the floor as slowly she stood up. She was doing everything in slow motion.

"Charlotte!" he was now shouting at her. "We need to go now, whether you are dressed or not, we need to get in the car!"

As they drove the 16 miles to the hospital, Charlotte's expression was blank, her eyes transfixed ahead of her. She was in another world. Charles was breaking every speed limit, but the journey seemed endless until they arrived.

"Charlotte, come on, darling!"

She didn't move.

"Charlotte, get out of the car right now!"

Never before had he raised his voice to Charlotte, but she needed to move, she was needed at the hospital.

Charles clenched her hand, almost dragging her through the corridors, as they reached the ward where Luke was.

Charles saw Robert and Anne as they walked into the ward, Charlotte like a puppet behind him.

"Charlotte, come on!"

Anne was distraught, her eyes were so swollen she looked like she hadn't stopped crying. Robert's tears started falling when he saw them both. Charles's eyes were drawn to Luke. Machines were helping him to breathe, and there was an oxygen mask over his mouth.

There seemed to be wires everywhere.

Anne reached out to Charlotte, but she walked past her mother directly to get to Luke.

"Luke, what have you been up to?" Charlotte began to stroke her brother's face, then gently brushed his hair with her fingertips. Anne tried to hold onto her daughter as she wrapped her arms around Charlotte's waist.

"Get off me!" Charlotte screamed at her mother.

Anne immediately removed her arms from Charlotte's waist, almost collapsing in shock, but Charles caught her with his swift reaction. The nurse came in at that moment and suggested perhaps they should spend some time in the family room. She was aware that it had been a long night for them all, and she knew that the day wasn't going to be much better. She reminded them that they would all need each other, and it would help if they could each regain some strength to help with Luke's recovery.

Charles began to lead Robert and Anne to the family room. Charlotte did not follow. She stayed with Luke at his bedside and continued to talk to him. Her eyes searched every inch of his body.

"Luke, come on, wake up, I'm here. Look at you. What are those idiots talking about, saying this is serious? You just have a scratch on your chin!"

Luke made no movement as Charlotte spoke to his lifeless body.

"I'm not listening to them, Luke, they don't know what they are talking about, you're my brother and I know you better than they do!"

Luke didn't stir. Nothing. There was no reaction.

Charlotte was becoming agitated.

"Wake up, Luke. Can you hear me? It's Sissy, I'm here right beside you."

Luke then all of a sudden began to speak. His voice was weak and shallow as he tried to respond to her voice.

"Sissy, watch the sky!"

The machine began a robotic call, red lights were flashing, Mayday! Mayday, cardiac arrest!

Charlotte was watching every movement as if in slow motion. Paddles were placed on his chest, the doctor was shouting, "Charge!"

Charlotte watched in horror as his chest bounced off the bed. As the doctor turned with the paddles in his hand, he yelled to the staff, "Get her out of here!"

Charlotte was taken by the hand and gently led away from Luke whilst the doctors continued fighting to save his life. Charlotte was still fixated on their voices and the sounds of the crash team continuing their battle to save him.

Charlotte was gently told to take a seat, and she never spoke a word. She focused on the clock on the wall, transfixed by the clock's hand as it moved. Tick, tock, tick, tock, repeated in her head. She was totally oblivious to anyone else in the room.

Suddenly the door opened. The doctor came in with a nurse.

"Luke has been taken to the CT suite, he is undergoing a CT and MRI scan to find out what's going on."

Anne collapsed into Robert's arms, and he was struggling to hold her. The doctor explained that Luke was still alive, he had pulled through, but he would be moved to intensive care, where he would have one to one nursing and specialist care.

Charles reached for Charlotte's hand, but she started screaming at him, "Let go! Go away, everyone, go away!" so he didn't know what to do.

Charles then spoke to Robert, telling him he was going outside to call his parents to tell them to come to the hospital.

Charlotte was left alone in the waiting room after the doctor appeared and asked for Charlotte's parents to go with him. Robert turned to Charlotte, looking for her to follow, but she just sat there numb. Charles, a few minutes later, entered the room.

"Charlotte?"

"What?" she snapped at him.

"Where are your parents?"

"They are with Luke."

"How is he, have they said?"

"He is dead, OK! He is dead."

"My God, Charlotte, what do you mean? The doctors said he had pulled through?"

With that, the nurse came in and asked Charles to step outside, where she briefly explained that he was not to worry, there had been no further news about Luke in his absence. The nurse was extremely concerned for Charlotte's wellbeing and warned Charles that she seemed to be in shock.

Charlotte looked like she had left her own body, and there was now only a ghost of herself sitting there.

Charles gently placed his hand on Charlotte's, but she abruptly pushed it away. To the outside world, they must have looked like two complete strangers.

Around 30 minutes later, Charles's parents arrived, and Charles stepped outside to update them on the situation. Charlotte saying Luke was dead was the last thing any of them needed to hear, and as yet, all they could do was wait for further news.

Charlotte herself was in deep shock and traumatized, so no one spoke. Each of them kept their eyes fixed on that damn clock.

Suddenly Charlotte heard screams, her parents' pain screaming through the ward. Charlotte burst through the doors. Her father was on his knees, begging God to take him and not his son. Anne was hysterical. Charlotte just stood staring at Luke.

Charles was told that the tests had now shown that Luke was clinically brain dead and that for the next 16 hours, the medical staff would perform brain stem checks. They told Charles that unfortunately, they couldn't see there is a different outcome, and after the checks had been completed, they expected to turn the ventilator off.

Robert pleaded with his son to wake up. Robert then screamed, "Please don't take another one of our children, please don't take our son!"

The doctor left the room to allow them to absorb what they had been told. He returned 15 minutes later and advised them to come back for 11.30 a.m. tomorrow, as the tests would then be complete.

Charles held onto Charlotte, his parents cradling Anne and Robert, as they walked along the corridors to the car.

When they arrived at Charles and Charlotte's home, no one spoke a single word, and they all just went to bed.

A light had gone out in their lives—one that would never light again.

As night turned to day, Charles didn't believe anyone had slept at all. The 22nd November 1994 would be the darkest day in their lives. The doctors confirmed that Luke had died. It was only the life support machine that was keeping his organs alive. With their consent, they would switch off Luke's life support. Robert and Anne just nodded. A nurse entered the room and asked if they could use Luke's organs, explaining this could help save another life.

Robert turned immediately. "No one will touch my son."

The nurse left the room as the doctor turned off Luke's life support.

Anne took a pair of scissors and cut some of Luke's hair, which she passed to Charlotte before cutting a lock for herself.

"Luke will always be with you, Charlotte!" Anne cried into her daughters' arms. Charlotte felt completely numb. She knew what was happening, but she couldn't control the situation. Was this a horrific dream?

Chapter 11:
Ashes to Ashes

1st December arrived quickly, and Charles and Charlotte's home was filled with mourners.

Charles was trying his best to hold everything together, with the help of his parents and Charlotte's friend Dawn.

Anne's brothers and their wives, cousins—anybody and everybody seemed to have congregated at Charles and Charlotte's home, and many people had traveled hundreds of miles to be there.

Charles's father approached him to tell him the hearse had arrived carrying Luke. Everyone stood up, and some people supported Anne and Robert in the car.

Charles held on to Charlotte's hand firmly and led her to the funeral car. The silence and somber mood were so overwhelming that the slightest gust of wind would have knocked any of them to the floor.

The church was filled with the music of "True Love Ways" as Luke was carried into the church. Soon it was time for the readings, and finally, it was time for Charlotte, who spoke of Luke's life. How she found the strength to speak, Charles never knew, but Charlotte was living outside of her body and felt like she couldn't control anything. It was as if she was living the reality of a dream.

The service seemed to pass so quickly, almost like a whirlwind, as Luke was led out to the strains of the song "He Ain't Heavy, He's My Brother."

Luke was laid to rest high on a hill. Charlotte chose that particular plot so that he could always see her coming up the hill toward him. She would never forget the last words he had spoken, "Watch the sky, Sissy."

This hill was going to be their special place where she could sit with him, as this was the closest point to the sky for many miles around.

The day had been as beautiful as it possibly could have been, and although everyone else went back to their lives within a couple of days and started to make Christmas plans, this was not the case for Charlotte's family.

Anne and Robert were all packed to go home. They needed their own space to try and come to terms with their grief.

Charlotte wouldn't talk to her parents except to say that it was her fault, everything was her fault. Luke would have been alive if it wasn't for her. If she hadn't been in hospital, and he hadn't had to come and help to look after her, he wouldn't have been there at that place at that time. She told Charles to go to another room or stay as far away as he could. She was poison, she was cursed, he should leave her. He could have another life, have children with someone else. She had killed their child. She screamed to God most nights, "Why didn't you take me?"

Robert and Anne heard her, but no one could reach her, and at the same time, her parents too were inconsolable.

Anne and Robert left, Charlotte watching from her bedroom window. As her parents turned to look for her, they noticed her watching them. Charlotte never even acknowledged them, and she turned away from the window without even a goodbye.

Charlotte sank deeper and deeper into a depressive state. Two years passed and Charlotte's behavior was now becoming increasingly irrational and erratic. She was constantly emotional and withdrawn, and no-one could get through to her. She pushed so many people away.

Charlotte was having a complete mental breakdown. She was doing crazy things, no one could stop her or reason with her. She spent most of her nights awake, sleeping through the day. She began to drink and started smoking. She was becoming obsessive in her manner and kept desperately seeking the ghosts which haunted her waking hours.

She would keep vigil at Luke's grave, pleading with him to appear. Charlotte was completely destroyed inside, tearing every inch of herself apart. Her grief overwhelmingly took hold over her body, and she seemed bent on destroying anyone who came to a fraction too close to her.

She had now become a person who wanted to destroy herself, as she was convinced that by behaving this way, God would take her. She would be punished, God would punish her and throw her to the devil. She suffered horrific nightmares, screaming most of the night. The pain in her head was uncontrollable at times, but still, she endured the torture she put on herself.

One night came when she finally pushed Charles to the limit. He had had enough, and he told her he was leaving.

He told her he couldn't physically take any more, so he grabbed his coat and left to stay at his parents' home.

"Good, good!" shouted Charlotte, and she then started screaming in their home.

"Good, everyone leaves me. I am glad you have all gone. I can't hurt anyone now, can I God?" she was screaming at the top of her voice.

Charlotte pulled the top off a brandy bottle and began drinking it neat. She started singing and dancing and turned the music up almost to the maximum volume, the bottle of brandy almost finished.

"I don't care, I don't care!" she was screaming and then singing again.

Charlotte's erratic behavior was at its peak, but suddenly she collapsed to the floor, unconscious. The music continued playing the same song, as she had put it play on repeat; "He Ain't Heavy, He's My Brother," over and over again…

There was banging at her front door, which grew increasingly loud. The noise from her house was driving the neighbors mad. However, unbeknown to the person banging, Charlotte was lying unconscious on the floor, and no one was there to do anything about it.

Charles had gone.

Soon the banging became more of a hammering.

It was Janice, their next-door neighbor. By this time, it was four o'clock in the morning. Janice could see that all the lights were on downstairs, so she peered through the windows, and saw Charlotte lying on the floor. Where the hell was Charles?

Janice knew about some of the personal turmoil Charlotte and Charles had suffered; the local press had covered the news of Luke's horrific car accident and the subsequent inquest in detail, but she hadn't known the extent of Charlotte's self-destruction until now. Janice, filled with panic, immediately ran back to her house, dialing 999 with shaking hands.

The ambulance, police, and fire service said they were now on their way, but Janice felt that she couldn't wait that long, she knew she needed to get in to help Charlotte immediately. She grabbed a heavy rolling pin from her kitchen and smashed the glass in the front door.

The glass smashed into a million pieces.

"Charlotte, it's Janice, everything is going to be OK!"

Charlotte was completely unresponsive.

Janice immediately placed Charlotte into the recovery position and began to check her airways, as the sound of, "Hello, hello?" came through the door.

A few minutes later, Charlotte was in the ambulance en route to the hospital, having her stomach pumped, and Charles had been informed.

Charlotte began to open her eyes. "Where am I?"

She didn't know where she was, the lights were so bright.

She then heard noises around her.

"Hello, hello, I can hear you!"

"Hello, Sissy!"

"Luke, thank God, Luke!"

Charlotte seemed out of breath as she spoke.

"I knew I had been in the middle of an awful dream, you would never believe me if I told you, Luke!"

"Calm down, Sissy!"

"Honestly, Luke, it's been awful!"

"I know, Sissy, we have been watching you!"

"You have, Luke?"

"Why have you been doing this to yourself, Sissy?"

"Luke, you died in my dream, and it was all my fault. Completely my fault. If I hadn't lost my baby and been sick you would still have been with us."

Charlotte's breathing was becoming erratic.

"The accident, all of it, I just couldn't cope anymore Luke, I couldn't cope. Thank God, it was a horrible dream!"

"Calm down, Sissy, you're going to have a panic attack!"

"Where the hell are we, Luke? Tell them to turn off those damn lights. I can't see anything other than these lights!"

Luke hesitated for a moment to allow Charlotte to catch her breath.

"Now, Charlotte, I want you to listen very carefully to me. I need you to slowly sit up."

"OK, Luke."

"Hold my hand Charlotte and walk with me."

As Charlotte began to stand up, she felt really dizzy.

"Wow, my legs feel like jelly, Luke!"

"Sissy, come on! We don't have much time."

Charlotte walked with Luke, each of them holding on to the other's hand, and Charlotte suddenly found that they were standing at her front door. Luke carefully opened the door.

"I don't know what's happening to me, Luke. Have I had a bang or something to my head?"

"Come on, Sissy, sit down."

"Where's Charles, Luke?"

"Questions, questions! Hold on a minute, Sissy!"

"OK, Luke, I hear you, bossy!"

Charlotte sat on her sofa as she looked around the room.

It was definitely her lounge, but it felt strange. It was her sofa, it was her home, filled with everything she remembered. Luke then came into the lounge carrying a tiny baby, wrapped in a beautiful blanket.

"There you go, Sissy, there she is, isn't she a beauty?"

"Oh, Luke, she is adorable, so adorable. Who is she? What's she doing in my house, Luke? I'm telling you, Luke, I feel completely spaced out here!"

"Charlotte, look closer, look at her face!"

In that instant, Charlotte knew exactly who the tiny baby was.

"Urrrhh!" Charlotte gasped.

"Yes, Charlotte, it's Courtney, your beautiful baby girl!"

Charlotte began to cry as she held her beautiful little girl in her arms, "My beautiful girl, my precious baby, where have you been?"

Luke just watched as Charlotte cradled her child.

"I'm so sorry, what's happened? I don't understand any of this, Luke, where have I been? Courtney is a newborn baby, I don't understand?"

Charlotte was now starting to hyperventilate.

"Calm down, Sissy, time is running out fast!"

"Time?" What did Luke mean?

"Where is Charles, where are Mother and Father, Luke?"

"Look out of the window, Sissy! Charles is there, mother and father too!"

"Oh, thank God, come on, Luke, let's go outside. Mother will want to hold Courtney, come on, or we will both be in trouble!"

Charlotte stood up and headed toward the door, about to go into the garden.

"I can't, Sissy, I have to stay here, this is where I live now, I'm part of the sky. I always watched over you, Sissy, every day, I never left you! It's not a dream, we are in heaven, Sissy. What happened to me wasn't your fault, none of it was your fault. We have only a certain time on the terrestrial plane, whether we are sent as a baby or even as a baby who has been miscarried. It's still part of a journey we take back with us to heaven. These are the lessons we learn. Time has no end here. While we were on earth, we each learned how the human heartbeats. We learned to love from the moment we entered the womb, to the moment when we died. We bring back with us the love we learned on the terrestrial plane. It's wonderful here, Sissy, so beautiful! I miss you all so much, but it was my time, and Courtney's short journey was her time. Now you have to choose, Sissy, you can stay or go back, but you are not meant to come yet, it isn't your time. We can see your pain here, but you cannot go back if you decide to stay. You had to be shown that none of these bad things were your fault, and you needed to know that we are here, and we will be waiting for you when your time comes if you choose to go back. I love you so much, Sissy. I will hold Courtney in my arms, and she will be here waiting for you when your time does come. I love you, and I need to tell you to go back. Look at the faces of the people who love you, Sissy, they are in so much pain. They are hurting too, go back, Sissy, tell them that it's wonderful here, and we are happy. Go and enjoy life, Sissy. Let them know I'm not sad, it was part of my journey. To have known love—true love—you also have to feel the pain, to know that your love is true.

"Look into their eyes, Sissy, go back to them, go back, they need you. I love you, my darling Sissy, watch the clouds, and watch the sky.

"Whenever you need me, I will be there. I will come back in your mind whenever you need me. Now go back, it's time. Get well, Sissy!"

"Luke, Luke… I love you, I love you. Courtney, I will tell Daddy about you, and he will meet you too one day. Hold her tight for me, Luke. I will always have you in my mind, I love you. Bye my darlings, bye!"

Charlotte turned to leave, as Luke waved her on, and they both had tears in their eyes as Luke walked back toward the light, cradling Courtney.

"Charles! Charles, darling, I'm here! Mother, Mother!"

Charlotte opened her eyes. Charles started stroking her head, "It's OK, darling, I'm here, I'm here!"

Charles explained to Charlotte that she was in the hospital and had been drifting in and out of consciousness for almost two days.

"That was some good brandy you drank, Charlotte!"

She had had alcohol poisoning.

"Darling, I saw Luke, I saw Courtney! I'm so sorry darling, I'm so sorry for everything!"

"No, Charlotte, I should never have gone and left you!"

Tears were falling from their eyes, as Anne suddenly spoke, "Please, could I squeeze in?" Robert was behind her. Charles hugged Charlotte tightly as the four of them cried. They would never be the same, but Charlotte had come back to them, and now they would try to rebuild their lives.

Charlotte told them about her meeting with Luke and Courtney, although they all thought she must have been dreaming. However, they felt that if that was what brought her back to them and gave her the impetus, she needed to seek help, if she believed it was real and it would help her to finally grieve, then they too would accept it.

Charles and Charlotte's parents agreed that perhaps it would be better if Charlotte never found out the truth about her real father, as she was so clearly emotionally fragile after everything that had happened. Charles had never kept anything from Charlotte, but now he was hiding their dark secret.

Chapter 12:
The Old Convent

Charlotte, with Charles's help, started counseling sessions.

She would chat with Anne and Robert most nights on the telephone, and slowly the four of them started to rebuild their lives.

Sometimes Charles could still see the pain in both Charlotte's and her parents' faces, and occasionally he heard Charlotte talking to Luke in her sleep.

Some nights, she would hear noises in their house and would be convinced it was Luke, and that he was with her and in their home because that had been the last place he had enjoyed before his tragic death.

Anne and Robert were arriving today. Charles had made a decision about something, but he wanted to speak to Anne about it first. Anne's advice would determine if he would then talk to Charlotte.

Charlotte was smiling at Charles. Their home looked and smelled wonderful as they awaited the arrival of her parents.

"Charles, have you set the table? Have you done the napkins? Have you lit the candles?"

"Charlotte, I do know what to do, and yes, I know how fussy your mother is. Hyacinth Bouquet!"

This was Charles's pet name for Anne.

"Charlotte, I swear, you're the double of your mother! But then they do say, look at the mother and you'll see how your wife will turn out!"

"That's it, Charles, I'm telling her when she arrives!"

They both laughed, as Charles was the ever-dutiful husband, and he did everything Charlotte wanted. He was a man who totally adored his wife. Charles was a beautiful man inside and out, there was nothing corny or crass about him. If Charlotte asked him for the world and he didn't have it, he would find a way to get it.

Charlotte was back on her feet now and taking pride in her appearance again. She still loved fashion, and her home looked as if it had been designed by an interior designer. She had an artistic touch and loved to be creative, whether it be with flowers, food, clothes, hair, or make-up.

Charles had never forgotten the moment he had first set eyes on her at her party, or the episode where they had met again in Harrods. She was his destiny, she was his partner on life's journey. The fact they could not have children together made no difference to either of them. The love they held for each other was enough.

"They're here, Charlotte!"

Charles opened the front door to greet them.

"Hello, my sweetheart!"

Anne knew Charles wanted to talk to her in private.

"Come on, Charles, I'll help you in the kitchen."

"Thank you, Anne, it's fine, I can do it!"

"I know, Charles, but you wanted to talk to me about something, perhaps now would be a good time?"

Charles hesitated before he began to speak. He felt uncomfortable mentioning anything regarding Luke, but he knew it would always be difficult. He always tried to be sensitive, but often he had the feeling that he was walking on eggshells.

"Anne, I think it might be good for Charlotte and me to move to a new house. Charlotte has been remarkable in her recovery and the progress she has made with her therapy…"

Charles paused, feeling a little flustered, "I feel it's for the best, but she is still having those dreams, Anne!"

"I see, Charles, and do you know where you both will go?"

"Yes, I do, Anne, I have seen the most beautiful house, and I think it would be good for her to have something new to focus on."

Silence fell between them as Anne absorbed the idea, trying to work out how best to advise Charles.

"It would be a new start, what do you think, Anne? Would you help me approach this with Charlotte?"

"Yes, of course, Charles!"

Anne knew he had not come to this decision easily.

"I also would like to know your feelings about us leaving this house, Anne. I would never intentionally hurt Charlotte, and I don't know if you also feel it, but I think Luke is here, too."

"Charles, if you feel it's right, then follow your heart. I don't need a house, or even a certain place to remember Luke. I will always remember him."

Charles sighed with relief. Anne smiled warmly at him.

"Let me try, I will speak with her and see how she feels about living somewhere else."

Much to their relief, Charlotte welcomed the suggestion, saying a clean break would be good, and confessing that many sad memories lived with her in this home.

The proposed new house was huge but an empty shell.

Charlotte felt a strange presence in the house, similar to the feeling in her dreams—as if there were people living in the house, but you couldn't see them. She could feel them drawing her in as if they wanted her to be part of the house.

The house comprised seven bedrooms, four bathrooms, two kitchens, two reception rooms, and an orangery. It had been built in 1880 as a convent, to house the nuns affiliated to the nearby Catholic Church.

The Church had had to sell the convent in the early '80s when they desperately needed funds to repair the church roof. When the convent was first sold, it became a hostel for single mothers. It was used as a safe place for mothers who found themselves homeless, or who needed to find a safe haven away from volatile partners and husbands. The hostel had been shut a while ago, and the house had been put on the market for sale again.

Anne turned to Charlotte,

"Darling, imagine what you could do with this—with your imagination and inspiration, it will look absolutely stunning!"

"I know, Mother, and it's only five minutes to the churchyard, look out the back, mother, the cemetery is just there!"

Anne knew that Charlotte visited Luke's grave regularly, but she didn't want to comment. Robert turned and spoke to Charlotte. "Looks like it could take a long time to get it in shape, Charlotte!"

"I know, Dad, but all these rooms!"

"Well, Charlotte, now you are a woman of substance, as you told me when you got off the train that Christmas in 1990!"

"No, Dad, I actually said I was a 'lady of substance!'" and they began to laugh.

Who would have thought that they could ever be laughing again?

Charles spoke with the agent and put forward an offer.

Charles was an only child and his grandparents had left their entire estate to him when they died, so money wasn't a problem.

Charlotte was so excited—it would take four weeks to be finalized, and then they would be in their new home!

Anne and Robert didn't want their daughter to be under pressure, or for the move to cause her any form of distress, so they helped as much as they could. Their home was filled with boxes and there were lots of arrangements to be made. Anne watched her daughter, who was now filled with motivation and expelling excitement. It had been a long time since her mother had seen her this way.

When it was time for her parents to go home, they hugged each other so tightly. This was the worst part: the goodbyes. Charlotte kept saying that she wanted her parents to live with her, but they would simply reply, "One day, darling!"

However, she knew they would be back soon, for they never stayed away for long.

Dawn had offered to help with the move, and Charlotte was delighted to have her help. Charles was up to his eyes with work, as his job had become increasingly demanding, and he was often totally exhausted.

Charlotte had known about the demands of his job when they started dating and she accepted it. Charlotte no longer worked due to her health, and she appreciated that Charles had provided her with a comfortable life.

Dawn was with Charlotte as the removal firm set to work. They worked alongside each other, and Charlotte was amused to see that Dawn could be rather bossy at times with the workers, but she knew that Dawn just wanted to ensure that the move went as smoothly as possible.

Charlotte chatted happily to Dawn as they arranged the furniture in her new home, remarking how strange it would feel to be sleeping in this huge old house. It was now evening, and everything was in its place. They had sailed through all of their tasks, working like two Trojans. They heard the door open as Charles walked in.

"No dinner? What on earth have you been doing all day?"

Charlotte turned—she was exhausted, "Don't push it, Charles!" as all three of them broke into laughter.

The week had passed so quickly, and the time came for Dawn to leave. They exchanged emotional messages as Dawn's train rolled into the station.

"I can't wait to see it finished!" Dawn shouted from the train as it departed the station.

"It's going to take forever!" Charlotte cried back, but she now felt like she had forever: she wasn't going anywhere! After all, it wasn't her time.

Five years later, the house was almost finished. Everything had been done, apart from the top room.

They had used stunning samples from Harrods to help fill this house, which was one of the perks of her beloved Charles working for the store.

Charlotte had felt comfortable in her home from the very start, but sometimes when she was alone in the house, she would feel the brush of someone passing her or hear footsteps going up the staircase.

"Hello, hello?" she would call, but no one replied.

Why would they?

Charles had bought a grandfather clock that he had seen in a local antique shop. He admired the richness of the mahogany and the striking design of the beautiful clock face. The pendulum would chime as the hour came, and Charlotte would set her day by it, as she never wore a watch. The watch her parents had bought for her 21st birthday was kept in her jewelry box.

Charlotte only wore her wedding ring and her precious gold locket which contained a lock of Luke's hair. Charlotte began experiencing things at night. She would feel someone stroking her face or pulling at her covers. Sometimes she would feel quite nervous, but she didn't know why, and she would snuggle into Charles without mentioning it.

Charles woke up on many occasions to find her sitting up in their bed, having a conversation with someone, but no one was there. Charles was becoming concerned.

Were Charlotte's nightmares coming back? Perhaps she needed to see her counselor more frequently. *Was the pressure she was putting on herself to make the house perfect exhausting her?* Charles wondered.

Charles was always so protective of her.

The one-sided conversations were now happening almost every night, but one night, things took a different turn.

Charlotte climbed out of bed and began to walk up the stairs to the top bedroom. The old convent was rather quirky in design, so perhaps it had stories of its own to tell. What secrets did it hold?

"Charlotte! Where are you going? Come back to bed!"

Charlotte was in a complete trance, was she sleepwalking? Charles stood back as he wasn't sure what to do. She slowly opened the door to the top bedroom.

Charlotte stood in the middle of the room for a few minutes, as the shadow cast by the moonlight reflected her outline on the wall. Charlotte began talking as she stood in the empty room.

"Hello, I am here now. Don't worry, everything will be OK, don't be frightened, please don't cry!"

Charles suddenly felt cold, shivers running through his entire body, as an overwhelming coldness filled the room. He needed to get Charlotte out of there.

As Charles tried to enter the room, he was struck by a powerful force preventing him from going forward. He stood in the doorway, completely powerless, as Charlotte began to sing in a soft voice.

"Hush, little baby, don't you cry, Papa's going to buy you a mocking bird…"

She was swaying from side to side as she sang.

Suddenly her singing stopped, and she began to walk toward him leaving the room behind. She walked straight past Charles as if he wasn't there.

Charlotte was now walking down the stairs, checking each door as she passed. Charles was behind her, he couldn't believe what was happening, and the house felt so cold.

Charles's eyes were drawn to the time on the grandfather clock. It was 2.26 a.m. He continued following Charlotte as she checked every room in their home. Every clock in every room said exactly the same time, 2.26 a.m., it was as if time was standing still.

Charlotte began to walk up the stairs again, "Ssshhhh, now, everyone is sleeping!" she whispered, as she passed the grandfather clock. The clock was still at 2.26 and the pendulum was completely still. Charles shuddered.

Charlotte was now back in their bedroom. She pulled back the covers as she laid herself back down and went straight back to sleep. Charles lay down next to her, still wondering what the hell he had just witnessed. He was completely spooked and never slept at all for the rest of the night. There was no way he was touching those clocks!

The morning rays came through their bedroom window, "Thank God, the night has now gone!"

Charles said as he headed downstairs. Charlotte was still fast asleep.

When Charles spoke to her about the events of the previous night, she had no recollection of even getting out of bed.

Charles set the clocks back to the correct time and decided to shrug it off. It was just Charlotte sleepwalking, he decided, she was having one of her dreams. Charles called their plumber that morning, telling him he wanted the heating checked. He was hoping that might explain the coldness he had felt in the middle of the night. He felt he needed an explanation for his own peace of mind if nothing else.

A few months later it happened again at exactly the same time—2.26 in the morning, so he decided he was going to keep a log. He was now beginning to question his own sanity.

The old convent carried on sending weird messages, and rousing Charlotte from her bed in the middle of the night. She was never spooked; she accepted the house for what it was. It was old and quirky and had a story of its own. She knew that life had existed in the house before them, and her philosophy was that no house ever became completely yours, it would always be borrowed.

Charlotte truly believed that a trapped soul could stay present in a home if it missed the timing of the light.

She always remembered her own few minutes in heaven, when she had had only a few minutes to decide whether she should stay or go back. There was nothing to be frightened of. She had seen for herself how beautiful it was, and how everyone was happy after they passed. Her own brother had told her that those who had passed were always around and were watched over by their loved ones. The noises that could be heard in the house sometimes were only them telling you they were there, or that you needed to be aware of something that was to come.

Charles could now sometimes hear the clanging noises or knocks at their door when nobody was there, but Charlotte was always reassuring to him when it happened.

"Charles, it's nothing, it is probably Luke letting us know he is here!" She was sure it was Luke, checking on her and making sure she was OK.

Anne and Robert were coming to stay one weekend and Robert was going to tell them about these incidents in person, feeling that it wasn't a subject he could discuss over the telephone.

Charles waited until Charlotte had gone to take a bath, as the rain pounded hard against the old windows. He began to draw the curtains in the lounge as Anne came through with a tray of tea and biscuits, ordering Robert to put more logs on the fire as it felt so cold. Charles never stopped Anne doing anything in their home, and he had always told Charlotte's parents their home was theirs too.

Once they were all settled, Charles told them of the events that had taken place, how Charlotte would frequently sleepwalk and talk to people who weren't there.

Robert laughed and suggested Charles put more water in his drink. Anne replied differently, "The spirits of the dead won't harm you, it's the living that does!"

As the evening began drawing to a close, they made their way to bed. Robert was discussing with Anne the conversation that had taken place earlier in the evening.

Robert felt a sense of uneasiness as he lay in bed. *This is stupid!* his thoughts were running wild, but eventually, he fell asleep.

He was awoken by the sound of Charles and Charlotte's bedroom door. Robert could hear the stairs creak, as cold air filled the room. He nudged Anne but she was fast asleep. Robert's heart was racing as he lay in bed. His eyes were wide open. Suddenly, a ghostly figure appeared, staring at him. Robert froze as the ghost enticed him to follow. It went straight through the door.

Robert began to follow the figure up the stairs to the top bedroom, where he could see Charlotte standing in the empty room.

As Robert began to enter the room, he was stopped, just like Charles had been. Stopped by a force so strong that he was unable to enter the room.

The ghost stood next to Charlotte as she began to sing, "Hush, little baby, don't you cry," and she turned, looking at her father. Charlotte was cradling a baby, "Ssssh, Jacob, please don't cry, ssshh," and she started to sing again, "Hush little baby, don't you cry." Light began to be drawn into the room, and the floor became covered in dead flies all around Charlotte's feet. Robert froze to the spot, fear running through his entire body.

He watched in disbelief as the ghost came gliding toward him, this time with heavy chains in its arms.

"Jacob!" he cried out.

As the ghost placed the chains over him, Charlotte followed and placed Jacob in her father's arms.

Charlotte began to walk back down the stairs, the ghost following behind her as the bedroom door slammed shut in front of Robert.

"Robert?" Anne was calling him, "What the hell are you doing?"

Robert made his way down the stairs, white as a sheet.

"Anne, there was a ghost, it was here!"

"Don't be ridiculous, Robert, your mind is playing tricks with you!"

Charles and Charlotte were out of bed and now standing in her parents' room.

"Are you OK, Dad? Mum, what's going on?"

"It's fine, Charlotte, your father thought he saw a ghost."

"Dad, it's only Luke messing about, I told you."

"That will teach you, Robert, you should add more water to your brandy!" Charles was trying to make light of the situation.

"Well, I don't know about anyone else, but I need a drink, cup of tea anyone?"

Charles suddenly noticed the grandfather clock had stopped. The pendulum was still. It had stopped again at Anne, Robert and Charlotte were now all sitting in the kitchen. Robert was still as white as a sheet as they began drinking the hot tea.

"Charles, I don't know about the nuns that used to live here, but I think you need to get a priest in!"

"Oh, Dad!" Charlotte replied.

"I think someone is trying to tell you something,"

Anne said quietly.

"Really, Mother, do you think so?"

"I don't think, I know!"

"Otherwise why would you say that?"

"Well, if it continues, I shall have no choice but to call the priest in. Something is definitely not right," Charles remarked.

Chapter 13:
Passing of Souls

Charles would never discuss the strange events that had been happening in their home with his own parents.

They wouldn't have been able to understand any of it. Charles and Charlotte had not seen very much of them this last year, as his father was now becoming housebound. Charles's parents were now quite elderly, and they could no longer drive, so Charlotte and Charles would pop over and see them, rather than have them travel and stay over. His mother had her own ways, and they were quiet people who did not mix much. Charles's father had a muscle-wasting disease, and he was becoming weaker. Charles's mother was a devoted wife and had been a wonderful mother to Charles.

Easter was soon approaching, so Charlotte had spoken to Charles's mother earlier in the week, checking on their plans for Easter Sunday. Her own parents would be with them this year, and she was hoping Charles's parents would join them.

"Of course, Charlotte dear, you know how fond we are of your parents. Perhaps you could all come to us for the weekend instead, it would be much easier for us all."

"Martha, darling, that would be wonderful! Charles has been working so terribly hard of late, and it would be lovely to have everyone together for Easter."

Good Friday arrived, and the four of them planned to leave early to beat the London traffic. Charles was looking forward to the break and spending time with his parents, as he knew his father's condition had worsened considerably—in fact, he was now completely bed-bound.

Finally, they arrived, and his mother greeted them at the front door. Charles's father, Sidney, was in the lounge. Charlotte thought again that life was cruel, as this poor beautiful man was now trapped in his own body. He had deteriorated a lot over the last seven years.

His body was wasting away, and now a skeleton of a man lay in front of them. Charles and Robert together helped his father sit up, propping cushions up behind him to support his body.

Sidney loved watching Dad's Army on television, as did Charles and Robert, so it was cheering to hear the laughter coming from the lounge.

Martha showed Anne and Charlotte around her garden, as her wonderful flowers now bloomed in the springtime sun.

As per both family's tradition, they only ate fish on Good Friday, so they all enjoyed the local fabulous fish and chips, followed by a game of Scrabble, whilst Martha sat by Sidney's side. As the evening drew to a close Anne and Robert thanked Charles's mother, and they leaned over to give his father a kiss on the cheek before they retired to bed.

Charlotte said goodnight too, as she was also quite tired.

Charles locked the house up for his mother, who was almost asleep on the sofa next to her husband. For Charles it was lovely to witness this private moment of his parents' enduring love Charles pulled back the cover and gave Charlotte a kiss, pulling her close into him. He heard his mother close her bedroom door, then he drifted off to sleep.

Suddenly, he was awoken by Charlotte—she was sitting up in bed. Charles felt frustrated as he searched for the light switch. Not again, what was she doing now?

Was she unsettled because she wasn't at home? Charlotte was out of bed and heading downstairs. Charlotte was obviously sleepwalking again.

"For Christ's sake, Charlotte!" Charles was desperate for her not to disturb his father, but she opened the lounge door where Charles's father lay in the bed.

Charles was close behind her.

"Charlotte, stop, you will frighten my father, for God's sake!"

"Sssh, it's OK, Sidney, I am here."

She lifted his hand and placed it into hers, as she spoke to him, "Go, it's OK, Luke is there, and he can help you, don't be frightened. I promise I will look after Martha until she comes to you, go now, follow the light!"

Sidney drew his last breath and his heart stopped beating.

"Charlotte!" Charles was now raising his voice.

"It's OK, Charles, I got here in time to help him pass!"

Charlotte was awake, she wasn't sleepwalking.

"What are you talking about, helping him pass? Telling my father Luke will help him so he wouldn't be frightened? What the hell are you bloody saying, for God's sake!"

Charles turned the light on as Robert and Anne appeared.

"It's OK, Dad, I'm here, Charlotte has been having bad dreams."

Suddenly Charles's eyes were drawn to the clock on the mantelpiece. The time was 2.26. Charles's face suddenly turned white as he approached his father's bed. His father had died, and the time of death was 2.26 a.m.

"I'm so sorry, Charles, he is safe now, and at peace."

Anne must have heard some of the commotion. She appeared and asked Charles if he would like her to fetch his mother, and Charles was grateful for the suggestion.

Anne had been here before, she knew what it was like to lose someone precious. Charles didn't even have the words to tell his mother.

Charles sat in the lounge alone with his father, while Charlotte made tea. Soon the undertakers came and took Charles's father away to the chapel of rest. Martha was broken-hearted. Her beloved husband was gone from her sight, but never from her heart and mind.

The days passed, and Charles became unusually withdrawn. He was frequently angry, and his manner was changing, especially toward Charlotte, as grief began to take hold.

Charlotte began making the necessary arrangements with his mother, ensuring that it was as painless as possible for her. Martha was grieving deeply for her loss of her darling husband; her soulmate was gone.

Charlotte spoke at length with Martha and in the end, suggested she live with Charles and her. Martha agreed that it was for the best.

Charles helped his mother collect some of her personal belongings, and drove her to their home, her home now.

He left Charlotte behind to secure the house, saying that he needed to get back to work as soon as possible.

Although this meant that he would be missing his father's funeral, they understood. Charlotte had known the pain of grief, as had her parents, so they were not upset about his behavior toward them.

Anne and Robert left after the quiet and dignified funeral. Charlotte had spoken of Sidney's life on behalf of Charles and his mother with grace and composure.

It was a difficult time for Charles. He buried his head in work, but he knew this was not the answer. His father Sidney had lived a full and fulfilling life and had been a wonderful father to Charles. Now it was his chance to show his respect for his father, and he was determined that he would now care for his mother. Charlotte supported Charles by devoting every second of her day to Martha. Charles, however, was behaving extremely coldly toward Charlotte.

"Charlotte!" She would hear Martha's cries, and frequently Charlotte would lay by her side, trying to comfort her through the night. It seemed as if Martha's soul had gone, and that she was giving up as if she just didn't want to live anymore.

Charlotte would drive Martha to the garden center to try to entice her with wonderful cakes and walk with her in the gardens. They listened to the music that she and had Sidney loved and shared, and she even took Martha back several times to visit her former home so that she could see her beloved garden again. Martha attempted deadheading the flowers and pruning the shrubs, but really, she was just existing, her spirit inside had gone.

Martha had lost so much weight. Charles came through the door one lunchtime and noticed that his mother's plate was untouched.

"Why is your plate still full? Why aren't you eating, Mother? This is ridiculous, you will die if you don't eat!"

Charles's tone was filled with anger.

"Charles, do not speak to your mother like that. She is not a child!"

"Carry on then, Charlotte, you obviously think you know best!" as Charles slammed the door.

"It's OK, Martha, he is just tired and worried about you. Come on, Martha, try a little for Charles!"

Martha's eyes welled up as she took a tiny bite of the sandwich. Poor Martha, she was so lost and withdrawn.

November was now here, and Luke's anniversary was approaching. Charlotte was expecting to have three days of hell. It didn't matter how hard she tried to put the trauma behind her, every anniversary she was still raw, and it would be even harder this year, with Charles losing his father at Easter, and his mother as weak as a wilting flower in the desert sun. The house had been quiet for a while though, with no episodes, and no sleepwalking—in fact, nothing out of the ordinary.

The sun was shining through the orangery when the noises began in the kitchen. The door slammed and as he heard the sound of footsteps. Charles placed his newspaper on the table,

"What is going on, can't I even read my paper in peace, what are you doing now, Charlotte?"

The ghost had come back and was now standing right in front of Charles. Panic was setting in his mind.

"Charlotte! Do you see that?"

"See what, Charles? Nothing is here, Charles!"

But Charles's mother turned and spoke.

"I saw him, they're coming, it won't be long now."

"Mother, really? You saw it too?"

"I did, Charles, and they are coming for me."

"Mother, please don't talk like that! Charlotte, what the hell have you been telling my mother, whatever it is, stop it at once!"

Charles's mother had if fact asked Charlotte many questions about such matters over the last few months, and she had spoken to her on many occasions regarding Luke.

Charles had no idea such conversations ever took place between his wife and his mother. Martha had even gone so far as to ask her; did she think there was an afterlife?

And Martha was well aware that Charlotte believed she had actually been to the other side.

Charlotte had simply replied, "There are things that have happened, Martha, that neither I nor Charles can explain—like all the clocks in the house stopping at 2.26 in the morning."

Charlotte told Martha how she totally believed in God, and that she believed there was a place that we go after we die. A place that held no pain, for it was a place of peace, a place where our loved ones were, and where we would all meet again.

"Ahh, Charlotte, my dear, I will see my Sidney again! He is waiting for me, for his sweetheart to be back in his arms again!"

That's where the conversation had stayed, for neither of them were up for telling Charles about what they had discussed.

A few nights later, Charlotte and Charles were awoken by a huge bang, which resulted in both of them jumping out of bed at the same time. Charles opened his mother's door to find her groaning in pain.

"What are you doing, Mother? What happened?"

"I was getting out of bed, Charles; your father was calling for me!"

"Come on, Mother, let's get you back to bed. You must have been dreaming!"

"I wasn't dreaming, Charles! And don't treat me like a fool, your father was there calling me!"

Charles was shocked at his mother's reaction, she had never spoken to him in a harsh tongue before in his life.

"Help me, Charlotte, stop dithering!" he snapped, taking his anger out on her. Martha screamed as he tried to lift her.

"Stay with her, Charlotte, and don't attempt to do anything!"

"OK, Charles, of course, I won't. It's going to be OK, Martha, Charles has gone to call for an ambulance."

Charlotte said reassuringly.

Martha was now in the ambulance, blue lights flashing.

This was an emergency, and they needed to get Martha to the hospital as soon as possible.

The doctors examined her carefully, immediately ordering blood tests and X-rays, which confirmed that she had broken her hip when she had fallen out of bed.

She was very weak, and her recent reluctance to eat hadn't helped Martha's body either. She was going to need an emergency hip replacement, but she desperately needed fluids first. Once Martha was stronger, they would operate later in the day. The doctor wrote a prescription for as much pain relief as her frail body could safely handle and told them that they would assess her again later that day to see if she was fit enough to go through the operation.

Charles's mother was taken down to theatre, and Charles and Charlotte paced the corridor, waiting for Martha to come out of surgery.

After five long hours, Martha reappeared through the theatre doors.

"Thank God! Why on earth did it take so long, Dr. Mohammed? You said the operation would take no longer than three hours."

"Your mother has been in recovery. I'm sorry it took a little longer than expected. The recovery team wanted to make sure everything was OK with her vital signs before they transferred her back to the ward."

Charles and Charlotte both slept at the hospital. It seemed as if the dreaded nightmare of the past might be about to begin again, as history replayed memories of the past.

Although Charlotte now had to focus on Martha rather than Luke, her brother would enter her thoughts, but she tried hard to distract herself in caring for her mother in law.

The nurses were wonderful to them, especially over these difficult days. One day, Charles brought a huge box of chocolates from the hospital shop as a thank you.

Suddenly, he noticed his mother holding her stomach as if she was in a lot of pain.

"What's wrong, Mum?"

"Charles, my tummy is hurting... I don't feel very well at all, it's probably nothing though, it will wear off."

"Martha, I think we should call for a nurse to check you over, you shouldn't be in this much pain!"

Charlotte called immediately for the nurse.

"OK, Charlotte, I am terribly sorry to be causing so much trouble!"

"Your blood pressure is high; Martha and your temperature are a little high too. I'm going to call Dr. Mohammed to come and examine you, just to be on the safe side."

Dr. Mohammed arrived promptly.

"OK, Martha, I am sending you for an X-Ray. I want to see what's happening inside your tummy. I will be back after you have had this done, and hopefully, we will have some answers for you!"

Once Martha was back on the ward, Dr. Mohammed reappeared.

"Martha, we need to take you back to the theatre, my dear, it looks like there is a blockage."

He gently explained to Charles that as his mother was still weak from her hip operation, the consent form was particularly important, as the operation could result in her fatality. As doctors, they had to offer the best care for their patients, and if there was a chance of correcting a problem they would try, as long as the patient was willing to take the risk. Martha understood and signed the consent form.

Charles and Charlotte were distraught but trying not to show it, as they led his mother back to the theatre doors.

Martha looked at Charles, her eyes filled with tears.

She gave him a gentle smile. Charles kissed her gently on the cheek.

"I shall be waiting here for you, Mother. Be strong for me now!"

Charlotte leaned over.

"Now Martha, remember that we love you very much, we shall be with you in mind and spirit, and waiting for you when you come out. Be strong, Martha, you will feel much better after this last hurdle."

Martha gave a little wave as the theatre doors closed.

Almost two hours had passed before the doors opened again. Martha was asleep, as the theatre staff wheeled her back to the ward.

Dr. Mohammed pulled the curtains. "I am so terribly sorry, there was absolutely nothing we could do for Martha; her stomach was full of gangrene. It had been attacking her for months while she hadn't been eating."

Martha was dying and wouldn't survive the night.

Charles and Charlotte were completely numb as they held her hands. Martha never awoke before she passed and went back to her husband's arms. And yes, ironically, Martha passed at 2.26 a.m. The date was 21st November, the same day that Charlotte's brother Luke was declared clinically brain dead.

Martha was buried on the same date as Luke. The only solace for her loved ones was that they felt it was her wish, she had wanted to go, and she lost her will to live.

Charles withdrew even deeper into himself. He was also drinking heavily now. Grief had overtaken him, and Charles was using drink to shut out his pain.

Chapter 14:
Pandora's Box

Anne and Robert's visits became more frequent, as did their phone calls. A frequent topic was "How is Charles doing, darling?"

Anne was becoming increasingly concerned. Although Charles had Charlotte by his side, he was suffering, trying hard to hide the fact that he was holding everything in.

Charles continued drinking, but Anne never feared he would hit or attack Charlotte. Anne loved Charles deeply and thought he was a beautiful son-in-law.

Although he could never replace Luke or even Jacob, Charles was like a son to them.

Robert had deeper concerns. From bitter experience, he knew that it could take a single second, one error of judgment, to destroy a family.

Anne and Robert would sit and watch Charles closely, as Charles downed his eighth or ninth can of strong lager of the evening. Sometimes Charles would start laughing at nothing, then fall asleep still holding a half empty can of lager in his hand.

Charles was still polite and caring, but they all knew this couldn't go on forever.

"Charlotte, do you think Charles would see a counselor?"

"Never, Mum, he just wouldn't, he would never open up to anyone. He holds it all in. He will have to get over this in his own time, we have to wait, the way Charles did for me, Mum."

"I understand, darling."

As the months passed, Charles did indeed seem to brighten a little. As the first anniversary of his father's death was approaching, he seemed fine and almost prepared.

When the date arrived, they all went to the graveside and shared fond memories. Thankfully, Charles's grieving slowly subsided.

*****

"Darling!" Charles called for Charlotte as he came through the door.

"How do you fancy a trip to New York? I have to go to work. It would be a nice change of scenery for you. You could explore the sights in the daytime while I'm seeing clients?"

"Wow! New York, Charles are you serious?"

Anne telephoned, as usual, that evening, and Charlotte excitedly relayed all the details of the forthcoming trip.

The trip came upon them so quickly. Charlotte took great delight in walking the grid of Manhattan, and one evening they even took a horse and carriage ride around Central Park. They explored the city at night together and viewed Manhattan from the Empire State Building.

Charlotte had Charles in stitches,

"Charles, how the hell did those pigeons get up here?"

They were on the 84th floor looking out toward Central Park.

"Are you really asking me that question, Charlotte? They flew, how else?" He burst out laughing, tears falling as the wind blew them down his cheeks.

"Well, I didn't think they could fly that high!" she replied. Charles just hugged her tightly as he turned her toward him.

"Charlotte, I love you!"

They had endured a journey together filled with happiness but also with deep sadness. God seemed to have given them a gift of empowering love. They had learned to love, but they had also known pain, hurt, and loss.

"Charlotte, my life would be empty without you!"

"I love you, too, Charles! As my mother would say, it's called togetherness!"

New York had shone the light back on them both. They had shopped, dined, and watched some of the shows on Broadway. It was now time to go back home to London, but they would always remember the amazing time they had had there. Charles and Charlotte came back stronger, ready to take on the next part of their journey together.

Charles wasn't drinking so much these days, and their home was quiet, now that Charlotte was no longer sleepwalking. The strange noises had stopped, and peace had come over their home.

One morning, as Charles was leaving for work, they had held each other tightly.

"Charles, off you go, darling, or you will miss the train, see you tonight!"

"I love you, have a good day, bye darling!"

Charlotte put the kettle on as she took the mail to the orangery.

"Right, coffee and let's do this, I wonder want junk is actually in this!"

She spoke aloud, but she knew they didn't have any bills, Charles was methodical with paperwork, and he paid everything from their bank account on time.

Charlotte was almost through the mail when an unusual envelope caught her eye.

"Miss Charlotte Andrews." Who was that for? That wasn't her surname, she was married now, and her maiden name was Hughes. No resemblance, other than Charlotte being the Christian name.

She looked at it again. The letter was handwritten, and it had a Welsh postmark.

Well, I don't know anyone in Wales! she said, talking to herself. Charlotte remained puzzled, but she put it to one side and carried on with the rest of the mail.

Charlotte's eyes kept being drawn back to the letter. It couldn't be for her, could it? It had to be a mistake, it was just weird. Only the Christian name bore a resemblance to hers, but as far as she knew, no one had lived here before who had been called Charlotte Andrews. And wouldn't the nuns be addressed as Sister?

Charlotte recalled Charles telling her that after the nuns moved out, the house had become a home for single mothers.

She was so intrigued, should she open it? Would it be wrong to open it? Perhaps it was someone trying to find one of the single mothers who had lived here, perhaps it was a sign? After all, this house seemed to draw Charlotte into its secrets. Was something going to happen? Charlotte took the mail to Charles's study.

Perhaps he would be able to shed some light on it when he got home.

Charlotte started preparing a romantic meal for her and Charles and placed flowers and candles in the center of the table. Charlotte's mind drifted back to their time in New York, and the wonderful evenings that had given them time to reconnect. New York had given Charlotte something that she would never be able to explain to anyone.

One afternoon, she had found the most beautiful gospel church just off Times Square, and she had ventured in, sitting quietly at the back, listening to the choir. God's voice was coming through every single muscle, controlling each vocal cord, as the singers expressed his word in the song.

This was on a different scale to her church; her Catholic Church was very intense. She tried to imagine her priest suddenly breaking out in song and shaking and waving his hands. The elders of the church would have thought he had gone completely mad! She smiled at the thought of the gospel singers. One day, New York was to become Charlotte's second home, although she didn't know it at that moment in time.

"Charlotte, darling."

"Yes, Charles, I'm in the kitchen!"

"Mmmm, smells delicious, darling!"

"Go and get yourself freshened up, dinner will be ready in 30 minutes! A nice glass of red will be waiting for you, alongside your rack of lamb! Oh, and Charles, I almost forgot—the mail, I have put it in your study in order, just like the dutiful wife I am!" she laughed.

"OK, darling!" and she heard his footsteps go upstairs.

"Charles? Charles? Come on, I said 30 minutes, not 45, dinner will be ruined!"

"I'll be right there."

"Charles, do the mail later, or take it to work with you, come on!"

Charles, unbeknown to Charlotte, had in fact quickly showered and then gone into his office, to quickly scan the mail. However, when his eyes came across the envelope addressed to 'Miss Charlotte Andrews,' his face turned completely blank, staring at the letter.

He had never betrayed Charlotte or her trust, but inside this envelope could be the dark secret that had been kept from her for so long. The secret which had been buried when her mother, Anne, had left Wales and the secret Charles had become privy to when he had married Charlotte.

Charles had been the one to deal with the legalities of their marriage, as did her grandfather with the registration of her birth, so they had managed to keep the secret from her then.

Had John Andrews died? How would anyone connected to him possibly have known where Charlotte lived? Charles was extremely worried; this envelope could be the end. They had come through so much and were finally happy again. Why did this have to turn up now?

They were opening up a Pandora's box if they opened the letter. Could he hide it? But he knew she had probably seen it.

"Shit!" he said aloud, "If I lie, the lie gets deeper, but if I tell her to open it, how will she react?"

"Charles?"

He almost jumped out of his skin as Charlotte entered the study.

"I told you, dinner!"

"Yes, darling, I was just coming."

Charles put the mail back on his desk, not knowing if she had she seen him holding it, or if she had she heard him talking to himself.

Charles followed Charlotte downstairs and sat at the dining table, the letter, and its possible contents running through his mind.

"Are you OK Charles? Is everything OK?"

"Yes darling, I'm just tired."

"Ah, perhaps you're still suffering from jet lag, Charles."

Charles began to clear the table and headed to the kitchen, as Charlotte's voice came through like a dagger about to stab him in the back.

"Charles, did you see that envelope? Strange, don't you think? I wonder who she is, Miss Charlotte Andrews? Perhaps you can do some research, and find out where it should be sent? I must admit Charles, I don't know why, but I was very tempted to open it!"

"Charlotte, go and fetch the letter, and we will open it."

"Really, Charles? This is so intriguing!"

"Yes, Charlotte, just go and get the damn letter!"

Charles's heart was racing as he sat on the sofa in the lounge awaiting Charlotte, wondering how she would react once she read it.

"Here you go, darling!" and she handed him the letter.

"Come and sit, Charlotte, let's get comfortable."

Charlotte grabbed a cushion and sat on the floor between Charles's legs. She loved sitting chilled like this.

"Come on then, Charles, I'm so intrigued!"

"Charlotte darling, I am going to tell you a story. It was one that was told to me some years ago, and it's very important that you listen to it all. I hope, darling, that you will understand the reasons and the consequences of what I'm about to tell you. It's about something that happened a long time ago."

Charlotte looked bemused, and she listened to Charles as he rewound her life to the time when she was in her mother's womb.

Then to the riverside, where Anne and John had made that agreement with each other, pushing aside God's hand of fate, and playing the devil and his advocate.

For you cannot go against the force of nature. If you try and play God, you will find that leads to a road of pain and heartache. Like Eve tempting Adam in the Garden of Eden, there are always repercussions in life, and lessons being taught by his hand. His hand of pure love: the maker and also the redeemer.

Charlotte could not believe what she had just heard from Charles's mouth.

"Robert isn't my father, Charles?"

So, she had a monster for a father, a man who didn't even want her to be born, all for his own selfish, cruel intentions? He was the spawn of the devil. How could he have treated her mother in this way? To think that her father wasn't actually Robert! Yet he had dedicated his life to her, he had brought her up since she was a small child.

He had worked his hands hard so that she could have everything, and he had given her all his strength when she was poor. He had given Charlotte so much emotional support and love, as well as anything else he possibly could give her. With his other two children having died, Charlotte was the only child he had left in the world, and he completely doted on her.

Charlotte couldn't have asked for a better father in the world. She realized how much how her grandparents must have helped so much to nurture her too before Robert had come along. No wonder her mother wrapped her in cotton wool!

"Charles, if that letter is from him—"

"Let's open it, Charlotte, and then we will know."

Charles opened the letter for her and passed it to her to read. Charles sat pensively as Charlotte read through the letter. She looked at him in complete disbelief as she passed the letter back for him to read.

*****

Dear Charlotte,

You may find this letter a complete shock. It was for me, too, when I found out I had a half-sister. My father is Dr. John Andrews, who was at one time married to your mother, Anne. My father knows I am writing to you, but he said it was completely my choice. Charlotte, I couldn't leave this world not ever meeting you or knowing anything about you. My name is Clara, I'm 24 years of age, and my mother was married to our father, ten years after your mother left Wales.

I was born a couple of years later. My birthday is on the 22nd of November. It has taken me over a year to find you, Charlotte, and my search for you was a journey that I couldn't give up, I desperately needed to find you.

I hope you can find it in your heart to write back to me, I don't care how long it takes but I will wait, even if it takes forever.

My father, our father, is old, and my mother has died. I will never forget that day, ever, when I found my mother dead on our bathroom floor. My mother died from a brain hemorrhage, and I feel totally destroyed inside, and so lost and alone. I miss my mother so much, her love, and her devotion.

That is when my father told me that I was not alone in this world, as I had a sister called Charlotte. I cannot believe they never told me about you. I knew nothing more about you, other than the fact that you existed. All I was told by papa was that it was probably best to keep that Pandora's box closed. I couldn't, Charlotte, I needed to find you.

Charlotte, I hope when you read this, that you understand how hard I have tried to find you. I'm not after any money, or a home or anything. I just want to know about you, who you are. You are actually my sister, I'm not an only child!

Years before I was born, my father had a terrible accident, and whilst he was in the hospital, he met my mother. She was his nurse and looked after him for seven months while he was hospitalized, and when he left, she continued to care for him privately at home.

My father had broken his neck and had had to undergo several operations. It took years for him to recover.

My mother was always someone who was dedicated to her job, and she had never given much thought to having children. She was in her forties when she fell in love with my father. However, she wanted children, and when I was born, I was deeply loved. Papa has been the most amazing father to me whilst growing up.

Despite this, I have a huge void in my life.

Yours,
Clara

*****

Charles placed the letter on the table. He wasn't expecting what he saw next. Charlotte's face was filled with rage.

"He has been the perfect father? Bastard! Bastard, I hate him, I hate him!" She was raging.

"I have a half-sister, lies, and more lies! Why all the lies, how could he have treated my mother like that?"

"I honestly do not know what to say, Charlotte, I am dumbfounded."

"He wanted me aborted Charles, he didn't want me to live! And then he goes and has another child! I will kill him, Charles, I swear I will kill him with my own hands!"

"Charlotte, calm down, darling, I know you're angry, but you'll make yourself ill!"

"I wouldn't be here if my mother hadn't fought for me! I wouldn't be alive, and we wouldn't be together, Charles! He destroyed my mother's life, then had another child with another woman!"

"Charlotte, it's a lot to take in."

"Yes, Charles, yes, a lot to take in, and I should have been told a lot sooner! Why the secrets? Why did you keep this from me? Why did my mother, my dad, my grandparents?"

Charlotte burst into tears.

"I'm not allowed to be happy, I'm cursed, and every time I smile or laugh, something happens, just like my parents!"

Charles held her in his arms.

"Charlotte, darling, they had their reasons for keeping it from you, you know that, and you know how much your mother and father have loved you. They have already lost two children, Charlotte, and you're their life! Don't walk away from them, Charlotte, it will totally destroy them. They were always going to tell you, but we had been going through our own personal grief with the loss of Courtney, and then Luke's death, and your breakdown, darling, you were so fragile. We didn't want to break you mentally, by giving you something else to deal with, we had only just got you back. In hindsight, Charlotte darling, yes, you should have been told no matter what, but please, darling, please try and understand!"

"This is just so unreal, Charles, my life is a lie!"

"You have to find it in your heart to forgive us, I know it's a lot to ask, but please darling, look deeper in all of this. Think of your mother's pain, think of your dad, you're his girl and no letter, no new revelations, nothing will ever change any of it! You will always be his daughter, don't break his heart, Charlotte, your mother's too, I beg of you for them both!"

Charlotte started to cry, as Charles held her in his arms.

"Come on, Charlotte, I will run you a hot bath, and get you a brandy, it will help with the shock."

Charlotte was lying in the bath when she heard the telephone ring. It would be her mother calling, she was as regular as clockwork.

Charlotte jumped out of the bath and grabbed a towel, wrapping it around her as she walked toward the bedroom, dripping water from her body. She could hear Charles talking downstairs on the telephone, so she quickly ran downstairs. As she walked into the room, she could see that Charles was reading the letter to her mother.

"Charles!" she shouted angrily at him.

"How bloody dare you! Have you not interfered enough?"

"I'm sorry, Charlotte, your mother rang and was surprised when I answered, rather than you, so I told her about the letter. I meant no harm! Here, you speak to your mother now."

"Charlotte!" Her mother began to cry.

"I'm so sorry, we should have told you, I didn't know how to tell you, I could never find the right moment. I didn't want to destroy us—we have been through so much, I'm sorry, Charlotte, so deeply sorry, I can understand if you never speak to us again!"

"Mum, it's OK, don't cry, it isn't your fault. How is Dad?"

"He is very upset, darling, you're his girl, he is scared he is going to lose you, he has loved you all your life, the same as if you had his blood running through your veins!"

Charlotte spoke in depth to the pair of them for the next two hours, with both of her parents trying to explain everything.

They went through the letter again.

"What do I do, Mum?"

"Charlotte, darling, you must do what you want to do."

"I hate him, I don't ever want to see him or know him. Dad is my dad, Mum!"

"I know, darling, and he always will be, nothing will ever change that. You must do what your heart and head tell you to do. But think also of Clara, she has had a shock…"

Anne paused.

"I suppose the stone man melted," Anne said, with a fierceness in her voice.

"I will write back then, Mum, but only if it doesn't upset you both. After all, it isn't her fault, and she has lost her mother—and the shock of finding her mother dead must have been so traumatic for her, Mum!"

"Our precious Charlotte, yes, you have our consent! Do whatever you feel you have to do."

They both cried again. Anne said she would telephone as usual tomorrow, and Charlotte put down the handset and headed upstairs.

Charles had been lying in bed wondering if Charlotte would shut him out, but instead, she wrapped her arms around him. She loved him and could now understand why he had acted the way he did.

Charlotte lay awake for most of the night, thinking of Clara. She was going to write back to her now. She was beginning to feel intrigued.

Chapter 15:
Blood Sisters

Dear Clara,

Where do I start? If this paper could hold the tears that have fallen since the opening of your letter, you would be in no doubt about the utter shock I have been experiencing, along with such feelings of pain. It is hard to believe the scale of the secrets and lies that have been held inside this so-called Pandora's box.

I am deeply sorry for the loss of your mother, Clara. I cannot even explain how I would feel if I lost my mother.

My mother, whose courage, strength, and most of all love, has made me the person that I am today. It was my mother and my wonderful dad's advice to write back to you, and I know that I am very lucky to have the support of my darling husband, Charles.

I was shocked to find that you were born on the 22nd of November, Clara, as that is a deep dark day for my family.

That is the date that I lost my beautiful brother, Luke. After a tragic accident, November 22nd was the day we turned his life support machine off. So strange to think this is the very same day my half-sister was born—a half-sister, who for so many years, I knew nothing of.

I am not here to be cruel or unkind, but now that this Pandora's box has been opened, I think you must hear my side of the story. You were the one searching for me,

Clara, looking for me and for the truth.

Here is the truth. My mother adored John Andrews when they made their pact against God, that they would not bear children.

He told her that it was his responsibility, and one which he would control, but he didn't. My mother became pregnant, Clara, on her wedding night.

When, one day, my mother fainted and was taken to hospital, they found out she was pregnant. Fourteen weeks pregnant to be precise.

Your perfect, amazing father, who is a monster to me now that I know the truth, didn't want me. I wasn't to live.

Dr. John Andrews wanted my mother to abort me! But she couldn't do it, and she fought for me to stay alive in her womb.

He walked out on my mother and broke her heart, taking his love away from her.

He couldn't accept me, Clara, he never wanted to have a child.

Can you imagine how I feel to find out that in fact, he went on to have a child? Can you imagine how my mother felt, on hearing that?

However, incredible as it may seem, my mother is now doing fine, fortunately, because she was lucky enough to meet and be loved by my dad.

Now, a man like that is what you call a father, and he will always be my father. I cannot, and will not, ever accept that he is not.

My mother's life has been one which has been masked with grief. How she has ever managed to get herself through life, I will never know. All I have ever known is my mother's strength,

She survived, and is still here, supporting me, despite everything. She lost my baby brother, Jacob. He lived for only a few hours, then died in my father's arms.

My brother Luke was born when I was ten. He died at the age of 21 after an evil drunk driver killed him.

Both of my parents have dedicated their life and love to me, and through all the pain, they have always told me to follow my heart and mind.

They gave their consent and blessing, Clara, for me to write to you, even though it was breaking their hearts.

Their thoughts were about you, and your pain, Clara, and the grief you must have gone through in losing your mother.

So OK, I don't know how this is going to work out, Clara, but I am writing, so I guess that's a start.

I am married to Charles. Charles is amazing, and my parents are too. I am an only child now. I have no siblings, as they are both in heaven. And yet, I have you. I'm intrigued, and I know need to know more. I would like to meet you.

I would like to see for myself why he chose for you to live and me to die! I wonder, too, what do you look like?

What's the color of your hair? Do you look like me? Is your personality like mine, or are we complete opposites?

So, I would like to meet you. I shall come to Wales next Saturday. We can meet at the Green Dragon Hotel in Swansea at two o'clock if this is agreeable with you.

Please only write back if this is OK. I don't wish to write anymore. I would rather see you face to face.

Regards,
Charlotte.

*****

Charlotte read out the contents of her hand-written letter that evening to her mother. Anne thought privately that it was, perhaps, a little harsh on Clara, who was after all, still a young girl. However, Anne wasn't going to comment, as this was Charlotte's choice, and it remained to be seen how Clara would react.

"Mum, are you OK? And Dad, this must be so hard for you too!"

Anne was resolute.

"Darling, I cut Dr. John Andrews out of my life the day he abandoned us in the hospital. He is dead, as far as I'm concerned, and holds no space in my mind. The hurt would be, Charlotte, if he took you from us."

"Never, Mum, never!"

The letter from Clara arrived, confirming the two o'clock meeting. She would wait in the foyer for Charlotte and would be holding a purple scarf that had belonged to her mother. Clara had also acknowledged Charlotte saying that she wouldn't want to meet their father and confirmed that she wouldn't put her under that pressure.

Charles and Charlotte began their journey to the south of Wales on Friday evening. Charles had found a beautiful hotel on the outskirts of Cardiff. They would travel the remaining part of the journey the next morning.

Charlotte brushed her long blonde hair, did her makeup, and finally was ready. She was dressed in a classic navy suit. It was like a job interview, rather than a meeting of blood sisters.

When they walked into the foyer, they were early, so Charles suggested they went to the bar. Charlotte had a glass of wine and Charles a cappuccino as they waited for the time to arrive. When 1:55 p.m. was showing on the clock, it was time for Charlotte to go back to the foyer. She now felt anxious. She didn't know how she was going to react. She was so much older than Clara, almost 37 now. Just at that moment, the hotel foyer door opened, and in walked in a young lady.

She was wearing a plain green coat, which was rather too old for her years, and carrying a purple scarf. Her hair, which was cut into a bob, was of the brightest copper tone.

Her face was very pale, and she had lots of freckles.

She was of a petite build and looked very fragile—like a porcelain doll, Clara thought, almost as if you held her too tightly, she would fracture, and break into tiny pieces. How different she was from Charlotte, they looked like complete opposites!

Charles and Charlotte stood up, as Clara walked across. Charles spoke first.

"Hello, are you Clara, by any chance?"

In a strong Welsh accent, but as quietly as a mouse, she replied, "I am."

Charlotte reached out her hand to introduce herself.

"Hello, Clara, I'm Charlotte."

Clara started to cry, as she wrapped herself around Charlotte. It was a meeting of two people who were both anxious and afraid. Two people who had been kept away from each other, for what some had thought was for the right reason. Charlotte froze. She wasn't quite sure what to do, but Charles took out a handkerchief from his pocket and passed it to her, and said politely,

"Shall we go to the bar? It's quiet, and you can sit and talk quietly."

They sat for a minute or so in silence. Clara then spoke,

"I'm so glad you came! I cannot believe I am here, finally meeting you, Charlotte!"

"Thank you, Clara!"

They talked and talked, and the hours flew by. It was almost 6.30 p.m., dark now, and the party revelers were coming out in force.

"Clara, it's getting late," Charles said, a little concerned about her.

"You must allow us to drop you home, the city is no place for a young girl alone in the evening."

Clara accepted the gesture with thanks. It would mean more time that she could spend with Charlotte. She was in total awe of Charlotte and was already fixated with her, and with everything she had spoken about, for she had heard about everything Charlotte had gone through.

Charlotte, in return, heard how this petite, reserved young lady, who was raised by an aging father and a middle-aged mother, had been brought up wrapped in cotton wool.

Clara shared her own depth of pain with Charlotte and explained how the loss of her mother had affected her.

Charlotte felt almost like a mother figure toward her, as although Clara was 24, she seemed a lot younger. Clara in turn, now understood why Charlotte had felt like she did about her papa, Dr. John Andrews.

Clara had read Charlotte's letter to him. His reaction was enough. He had sat extremely quietly in his chair and never said a word to Clara. He absorbed Charlotte's words, her anger, and her hatred toward him, and he felt that she had every right to feel that way.

As they walked toward the car, Charlotte suggested Clara sit in the front, as it would be easier for her to give Charles directions to drop her home. Both Charles and Charlotte had found the Welsh spelling of the roads quite difficult, and since Clara was Welsh, it would be much easier for her. Suddenly, Charlotte realized with a jolt that she was actually Welsh herself.

They drove for 40 minutes through the dark countryside. They were heading deep into the Welsh valleys. The roads were dark now, and the only lights came from tiny cottages nestled in the hillside.

"Charles, there is a little side road to your right in a minute, you need to turn down there. This leads to where I live. Actually, Charlotte, it's where both our mothers lived. Papa and I live in the big house now, as granny and grandpa Andrews died several years ago."

The road came to an end where two large iron gates stood.

Charles unbuckled his seat belt to help Clara open the huge gates. Charlotte was peering through from the back of the car. Her mother had now told her the full story of Dr. John Andrews, but she couldn't believe she was here at his house. She was going back in time to the place where her mother had lived and had created Charlotte in her womb.

Charlotte had butterflies in her stomach and felt anxious and almost frightened. Clara and Charles got back into the car and Charles continued to drive with care, as the road was scattered with potholes.

Charlotte noticed a few little flint cottages either side of the road, then a much larger cottage on the right.

Clara turned to Charlotte,

"This is where my papa lived when he was married to your mother, Charlotte. Would you like to stop and see it?

There are no lights working, though. In fact, it has never been lived in since your mother left. Papa wouldn't let anyone touch it. He moved into the big house with Granny and Grandpa after that."

Charlotte was intrigued.

"I need to stop Charles, I want to see it!" Charles stopped just in front of the cottage and put his headlights on full beam. It was so dark, it was actually quite haunting.

Clara put out her hand to Charlotte,

"Come, Charlotte, let me show you!"

Charlotte's heart was racing. Her mind was filled with the stories she had been told by her mother, and fear started rushing through her entire body at that point.

Charles was right by Charlotte's side,

"Are you sure, darling, it's been a long day and I think you really have been through a lot today?"

Charles was, as ever, frightened that Charlotte would relapse and that her mind would break again.

"Yes, Charles, I am here now, so I need to see it. I think I will regret it if I don't. I need answers, Charles."

So there in front of the cottage stood three people whose lives had been affected long ago by the decision made by two lovers. Two lovers who had believed that the journey of life was theirs alone to decide. A journey they willfully altered when they agreed to stop the hand of fate, and the hand of God, by using contraception.

Their love had been a joining of two hearts between a man and a woman. This love they had for each other, though, was completely different from a father's love or a mother's love. Love for a child grown from God's empowering love and his teachings was no comparison.

Her love for this man had simply been naive young love.

Both of them had paid heavily back to God for the sin of rejecting his gift of love. They had lost the love that they had shared together, and each of them had had to learn the pain of loss after the creation of love. Pain, darkness, and rain.

But Charlotte was alive, and she was standing here at the house where God had sent his gift to John and Anne, a gift that John had wanted to refuse, but Anne couldn't.

Charlotte was God's precious gift of love.

Charlotte began to cry. This cottage was meant to have been the start of her mother's life, filled with an enduring and everlasting love. This is where she was created.

"I'm sorry, Charlotte, I didn't mean to make you cry. I didn't want to lie, but I wanted you to know."

"I'm OK, Clara."

Charles then spoke, "It's been a very long day, Clara, and a very emotional one. Come on, Charlotte, let's go back to the car and get Clara home, this has been an extremely difficult day for you both."

Charles noticed in his mirror that Charlotte was looking back at the cottage from the back window, as they approached the mansion.

The mansion looked almost derelict until they saw some flickering light coming from a few of the windows.

"Wow!" Charlotte was blown away by the scale of it.

"Clara, how do you cope with living here, it's so far from anywhere?"

"It's a little overwhelming at first glance, Charlotte, but you do get used to it. We have staff, and Papa has a driver. We don't use much of the house unfortunately, Papa has let it get in a bit of a bad state, I'm afraid."

As they arrived at the front of the mansion, they could see big stone pillars supporting the porch, and there were lights on either side of the huge oak front doors.

"Charlotte, would you like to come in? Would you like to see inside? You could see our family photos of Granny and Grandpa, and of Great-Granny? Our great granny Roselyn was a beautiful ballerina—she traveled all around the world, and would always take her red dancing shoes, her beautiful red shoes with her. I've heard of these shoes, but I've never seen them."

"Ahhhhh, no way! The red shoes, my red shoes, mother's red shoes! The ones I wore on my 21st birthday. My brother Luke even played and danced in them too!"

Charlotte was now even more intrigued—this was her history, and this house and this family was part of her—a family that she had had no idea of, or knew anything about, until Clara's letter.

"Charlotte, I think you have had enough for one day!"

168

Charles was still trying hard to protect her, but she didn't listen as she was desperate now to go in, she needed more.

"Come on, Charles, we have to go in!"

Charles took a deep breath, got out the car and helped Charlotte to the front door.

What was she doing? He had never imagined that they would be doing this.

Clara opened the huge oak doors,

"Come on, Charlotte, follow me!"

They entered the huge mansion with Charles following behind. Charlotte was drawn to the rich mahogany boarding which protected the huge stone walls in the entrance hall. She breathed in the deep character of the house—the smell of fireplaces burning logs that had been keeping this magnificent building warm for centuries.

Huge chandeliers hung from the ceilings, and although the parquet flooring was worn, it glowed with a light sheen from where it had been polished over the many hundreds of years. There were large vases on pedal stools, some of Chinese—possibly Ming in origin—and huge oil paintings hung from the walls.

The heads of stags that had once grazed the hillsides of the Welsh valleys hung in prominent positions from the walls. Charlotte also noticed some rather awful stuffed animals, all of which were free-standing.

Two large antique clocks which had been telling the time for decades were standing imposingly in the hall.

The atmosphere of the house was drawing Charlotte is like a magic spell.

As they walked the magnificent hallway, large mahogany doors appeared in the wooden walls. Were they secret openings? Where would they lead? And what lay beyond those doors? Dare she touch the handle and walk-in?

This time it was Charles who gasped.

"Wow, look at that staircase!"

Charles had worked for Harrods for many years, and had been in some magnificent homes, but this staircase was huge. It was split into two sections at the first level, one to the right and one to the left. A large tapestry hung in the center, with two bronze sculptures at either side.

Charlotte was drawn to an astounding fireplace. The beautiful black cast iron surround complemented the open grate. The fire was fully ablaze with large logs that crackled loudly as embers fired onto the grate.

"Isn't this beautiful, Charles?"

"It's very impressive, darling." Charles was feeling rather uneasy about being there.

"We are in here!" Clara spoke gently as she turned the handle and the three of them entered the library, revealing another huge fireplace that was similar to the one in the grand hallway.

Beautiful tapestry rugs covered part of the wooden floor and three huge chandeliers hung from the ceiling.

The top half of the walls were covered in tapestries, telling stories of kings in armor holding shields and swords, while ladies in fine attire gathered around. The room was utterly breathtaking.

Four large windows filled the room with daylight, and tall bookcases, filled with thousands of rare and precious books, lined the remaining walls.

These walls held centuries of memories for the family's predecessors—predecessors who Charlotte was only now beginning to realize were part of her history too.

Clara told Charlotte and Charles to relax and make themselves comfortable, as she pulled a large rope by the fireplace.

"Charlotte, this is your home too, feel free to look, touch or ask me anything. I am sorry that you never had your childhood here, we would have had so much fun playing here together!"

Charlotte's eyes began filling with tears, as the door opened, and a middle-aged lady dressed in a black and white uniform entered.

"Good evening, Lady Clara, how may I be of service?"

"Hello, Daisy! Charlotte, Charles, would you care for some tea?"

Daisy curtsied as she left the room with Lady Clara's request.

"It truly is a magnificent place!" Charlotte said to Clara.

Charles, too, was being drawn in like a magnet to its splendor, as Daisy knocked and entered the room, carrying their teacups on a tray.

Clara began to satisfy Charles's interest in the stately home, explaining that there were 19 state bedrooms, all with private bathrooms. Every state bedroom had its own unique style, and granny had taken great pride in her role in the refurbishment in the early seventies. Clara took them into the splendid picture gallery and told them that the room could accommodate a banquet for two hundred people. She explained that her grandparents used to hold parties there.

"This is the room where my mother must have fallen during the party!" exclaimed Charlotte.

She had been told by her mother about the party held at John's parents' home, the night Anne was wearing her red dress and the beautiful red shoes. The night she had fainted and been taken to hospital, where she had found out she was expecting a child, and when, the following morning, Charlotte was to be taken from her mother's womb.

Charlotte was quiet for a while but roused herself as Clara told them more about the family and the house.

Clara showed Charlotte many old photographs of her family, including her grandmother and grandfather. Charlotte bore a remarkable resemblance to her grandmother.

"Who is that, Clara? She is beautiful!"

"That's our granny Beatrice, Charlotte!"

A huge portrait hung in the library of Beatrice, portraying her as a tiny dancer—and she was wearing the legendary red shoes! Tears fell from Charlotte's face as she listened intently to their family history.

At one point, Clara stopped in her tracks and looked at Charlotte, amused. She informed Charlotte that she actually held a title. Officially, she was a lady and not a Mrs.! Charles was totally perplexed by this declaration.

"I thought your father's name was actually Dr. John Andrews, so surely that cannot be right?"

"Charlotte, papa's parents, our grandparents, were Lord and Lady of Dwyfornywn. So indeed, Charlotte you are by law a lady, Lady Charlotte Dwyfornywn.

That's why it took me so long to find you."

Charles was worried for a moment, but he knew that Charlotte's birth certificate said Dr. John Andrews, so he didn't need to worry that his marriage might be illegal.

"Well, Charlotte, that revelation is definitely enough for one day, we need to get back to the hotel now, darling!"

"Yes Charles, of course." Charlotte was totally dumbfounded as they stood up to leave.

"Thank you, Clara, it has been so much to take in—and I'm sure you must be feeling quite overwhelmed yourself. I promise to write when I am home, but I hope you can understand it is going to take a long time for me to adjust to this! However, you must know that I'm here for you, and you'll never need to feel alone again. Both of us are opening up pathways that neither of us have explored before. Pathways, Clara, in which people can get hurt—and my mother and father have had so much pain in their lives, I hope you can understand why I want to be careful not to hurt them. Maybe one day you could visit us in London? This isn't goodbye, we just need to take it slowly and carefully."

"I understand, truly I do! I know I have you, and I'm not alone. When papa eventually does leave me, I won't be frightened of feeling like an orphan, now that I have a beautiful big sister waiting for me!"

Tears were falling from her sweet face, as Charlotte, without the slightest hesitation, embraced her in a warm hug.

"Come on, ladies!" Charles prompted briskly, as he hated nothing more than seeing women cry—he was such an old-fashioned man at heart.

Charlotte and Clara walked hand in hand back through the grand hallway, heading toward the large oak doors when suddenly Charlotte saw a figure of a man at the top of the stairs. The figure turned, alerted to the sounds of voices and footsteps on the wooden floor. As their eyes met, he looked directly into Charlotte's eyes. He was a tall thin man with silver hair and an overwhelmingly handsome appearance. He was in his early eighties. No, it couldn't be, could it? Yes,

Charlotte suddenly knew it instinctively, this was her biological father.

The shock must have been overwhelming for John too, as suddenly he stumbled on the staircase and began to fall back down the stairs.

"Papa!" Clara's screams echoed throughout the house. Charles's swift reaction caught hold of him just before he hit his head on the staircase. He was hurt but he was alive. Charles helped the decidedly frail John carefully down the stairs. He was clearly still in shock and trembling as Clara approached her father and began stroking his hair.

"Papa, I'm here, Papa!" Tears were flowing down her face.

"Papa, you're hurt, I thought you were going to die there, I thought I had lost you!"

"Clara, I'm OK, there's still life in your old papa yet!" as John tried to stand steadily on his feet.

Charlotte fixated on him, and he looked back at the daughter he had never seen, the creation of love he had tried so hard to ensure would never breathe or exist in his world.

"I am truly sorry, Charlotte, for everything, there are no words, there is nothing I can do or say to you to explain my

174

actions. I regretted them deeply when your mother left, and I closed up and tried hard to shut her and you out of my mind and heart. Please tell your mother I am deeply sorry for all the pain I have caused her and tell her that I never stopped loving her."

"Are you kidding me?! I think the bang to your head has made you quite delusional!"

"Charlotte, don't be cruel, let the man explain! You wanted answers, and he is trying to give you them now."

"Well, his answers have been a long time coming!"

She replied to Charles, before turning to confront her father.

"If you had your way, I wouldn't be breathing!"

"Charlotte, please let me try, I was wrong, I made a vow and I broke it. Clara knows the truth about the way I feel concerning what I did, and I know that nothing can make up for it. I know you hate me, Clara showed me your letter. I'm sorry, I can't explain, and I can't turn back time, I think my heart must have been made of stone. I had never felt love before, or what I believed to be love until I met your mother. This households you firm, and when I was a child, I felt that I was always on duty as a son. My parents sent me away to boarding school from a small age."

"And is that your excuse, Dr. Andrews?"

"No, it's not an excuse, but as the heir to the family estate, and a lord from the day of my birth, I was taught not to show affection in public, and neither of my parents would either, they thought it was unbecoming. Mother and father had the duties of the estate to uphold, many social parties were given, and I felt I was used their trophy, 'the future heir.'"

"Can we possibly get your father a chair, Clara, he looks a little weak standing, perhaps he should sit whilst he speaks with Charlotte, I would hate for him to fall again."

"Yes, of course, Charles, silly me!"

Charlotte waited pensively for him to continue.

"My parents were always busy, and unfortunately I took that for pushing me aside. I never wanted a child to feel the way I did, but instead, I know now that what I did was so much worse. For that, I have lived all my life in pain and heartache. Clara's mother, and then Clara, came along years later and opened up my heart again to love, but by the time I realized the full extent of the pain I had caused, your mother was living her own life, and I couldn't bear to cause her any more pain. I had to live with what I had done. I shall have to face God and accept my punishment for what I have done to both of you, Charlotte, when I am taken from this world."

Charlotte now had tears rolling down her face. This wasn't the explanation she had thought she would get and now didn't know what to do, or how to react.

"Please, Charlotte, I am not asking you to do this for me, but for Clara! She is innocent, so please, one day come back to what belongs to you and to Clara!"

John then stood up and took hold of the banister. He began to walk back up the stairs, but he stopped and turned.

"Charlotte, you are so beautiful, and the image of your mother. I'm so glad she fought for you to be born. My punishment will always be that I have seen the beauty of your face, a face that I created with my beautiful Anne. and now I know that this is a face I will never see again, because of what I did!"

Charlotte watched him go from her sight, as her tears fell, and her heart ached.

For now, she just didn't know how to think about all of this, but at least she had her answers.

Charles directed her to the car. She was exhausted from the day, and from the past eight days since she had received the original letter. Now she was feeling emotionally and physically drained.

They hugged Clara as they said goodbye. Clara knew she might never see Charlotte again, not until time could heal her heart and she was able to fully deal with the revelations. As they waved farewell, Clara knew she would be happy to have any contact from Charlotte, even if only by letter.

Chapter 16:
The Healing of a Broken Heart

Charlotte slept most of the time for two weeks. When she did awake, she didn't stay up for long, and she would only eat a little food. She never spoke to Anne during this time. Charlotte needed time for her mind and body to absorb the shock of the recent events that had taken place. She needed answers from her head and heart, as to what she should do. This would be her decision to make, and no one else's. Charles had kept Anne and Robert informed of every detail, and they agreed they would be led by Charlotte.

When Charlotte finally had the strength back in her body and mind, she decided she would write to John.

She knew that she had to piece her heart back together and find peace again in her mind.

She felt that she wouldn't become sick again this time, as she would always have the moment she had shared with Luke and Courtney on the 'other side.' She was determined that she would live life to the full now and get herself well.

"Hi, darling, how are you feeling this morning?"

"I am fine, I am up and dressed! I was just about to pour myself some fresh coffee, Charles, and write to John."

"Really! Wow! I wasn't expecting that, Charlotte, but I am glad that you feel you need to do it."

"I do, Charles, I'm fine, don't worry! I shall call mother tonight as she is probably wondering how I am doing."

"I have been keeping them informed so that they wouldn't worry too much. They are fine and happy to go with whatever choices and decisions you make. I love you, Charlotte!"

"I am ready now, and clear about what I am going to do, there is nothing to worry about. Could you call mother to let her know I am feeling stronger, and ask her to call me at the usual time please, Charles?"

Charlotte made herself some fresh coffee, and as she began to write, the sun came shining through the lounge window. She looked up at the sky and felt the love beaming through her, exactly as if Luke was right beside her, sitting with her on the red oxblood sofa.

The ink flowed on to the paper, as her heart opened to write to John, explaining her decision.

*****

Dear John,

Please pass on my good wishes to Clara. I am sorry I didn't thank her before now for meeting up with me. I am sure you can understand that the whole event must have unraveled emotions for everyone. I am glad that I came, and I can understand the situation much clearer now after my visit.

I am sorry, John, regarding your upbringing, and your reasons for not wanting to have a child who might have to endure the same inflictions of pain that you endured.

You were adamant that if a child of yours were to be born, they would feel as you did because of your own feelings about your childhood, and the nature of your upbringing.

I am grateful that once you and my mother separated, you didn't disrupt my mother and father's life or mine, and I am able to say that apart from illness, I had a lovely childhood. However, I and my family did suffer immensely on my brother's death, and on the death of my own daughter.

I think of Clara and see an innocent young girl who has lost her mother, who has also felt the same type of grief as me. However, I hope you understand that I cannot see you—I cannot say forever, because who knows what the future will hold—but when you have passed, I shall take the decision with Clara on Garthmyl when the time arrives. I shall always be there for her—for that, you will have my solemn vow.

Please enjoy the time you have with Clara, and don't let my visit be a reason to shut the world out. I forgive you.

Maybe one day we will meet again, who knows? But for now, this is my response to you, and this shall stand as my letter of forgiveness, so that you can find some peace, both in your heart and your mind.

Please ask Clara to write. We shall keep in contact and somewhere, someday, we may find a time to reconcile and join our hearts together. So, let time heal now, John. I wish for your heart to mend.

Regards,
Charlotte

*****

"Hello, Charlotte!" It was Anne, calling on the telephone.

"How are you? Hope you're keeping well! Dad sends his love."

"I am fine, Mother, honestly! When are you and Dad coming to visit? I miss you both so much, and wish you lived closer!"

"Well, Charlotte, we have some good news for you, but we wanted to wait until you had dealt with John and Clara. I am so very proud of you, darling!"

"Thank you, Mother. I suppose Charles let you know what I said to John in my letter?"

"Yes, he did, darling, but the past is the past, and the present is now. Everything is out in the open, no more secrets! And you have forgiven us, your heart is so pure, my darling!"

"Come on, Mother, don't keep me in suspense! What's the news?"

Anne drew a deep breath; would she want her and her father now after all that had happened?

"We want to sell the house, darling, and spend the rest of our days by your side! You have asked us for years, and we weren't ready, but we feel that we are ready now. Do you still want us?"

The phone went quiet as Charlotte absorbed the information.

"Mother, of course! That would be wonderful—finally, we can spend every day together! The house is easily big enough! Wait till Charles hears! He is going to be so excited!"

Their house sold within 24 hours of the board going up outside and advertised online. Both Charles and Charlotte were not at all surprised, as their home was beautiful. They would be moving around November.

Christmas would be magical, Charlotte thought, *and from now on, her parents would never have to leave again.*

Charlotte called in the decorators to redesign the top bedroom, as this would give them privacy. Robert was a little hesitant, reluctantly admitting that it was because of his encounter with the ghost that awful night.

However, there had been no more interactions with the ghost and they both felt that redecorating would help.

In the end, moving day was changed to the 3rd December, so that they would be clear of Luke's anniversary as well as that of Charles's father. All of them wanted this to be a happy start—as Anne told Charlotte, "New beginnings!"

After all the commotion of the move, they were finally in! Robert gave the removal men a generous tip, as they had been wonderful. Finally, they could all relax and enjoy a welcome beer—"Totally for medicinal purposes to ease the aches and pains!" laughed Anne, as she and Charlotte clinked glasses.

"Can you hear the pair of them, Charles? We are going to have to stay strong—the twins are together, heaven help us!"

"Ahh, Robert, we probably won't see them for dust!"

Charles and Robert chuckled together as they enjoyed their cold, refreshing glass of Stella Artois.

"Mother, I have hung everything away now—what about your photographs, etc.? Would you like me to arrange your ornaments? I think you should, Mum, as I want you to feel straight away that it's your home now."

"OK, my darling, I am just glad we are with you, and we can spend the rest of our lives together! Me and my girl! Oh! And Charles and your father, of course!"

They both burst out laughing. The house was filled with joy and laughter. The evening was drawing in, so a feast from the local Chinese was ordered.

"Charlotte, shall we do something different for Christmas this year? I have always wanted to go to Hawaii and California—we could go for Christmas?"

Charles nearly dropped his glass of Stella. One thing you could count on Anne for was tradition, and Charlotte was identical to her in this way too. Robert's ears pricked up, and a huge smile spread across his face.

"Anne, shall we give it to them now?"

"What's going on here, Dad? What are you and Mum up to?"

"Yes, Robert, I think I am going to burst if we don't!"

Robert went to his old brown briefcase. Her father had had that case for years and treasured it. Charles had bought it for him one Christmas, years ago.

"Well, Charlotte, darling, our precious girl, this is yours! We want you to have some of your inheritance now. Since the house is sold, we don't need all this money. We want to travel, and you have paid for so many of our holidays! With this money, we can all do whatever we want!"

"Are your serious, Mum? Dad? Don't be stupid, we don't want your money, we're just happy that finally, you're living with us!"

"Charlotte, please take the check from your father. That's the end of it! Now also the tickets, Robert!"

"Yes, darling, I was just getting them out too!"

Charlotte was given a check by her parents for the sum of £350,000, as well as tickets for them all to fly to Los Angeles then onto Hawaii, leaving on Christmas day.

Charles and Charlotte were overwhelmed by the gesture of complete generosity, and the thought of their upcoming trip.

Charlotte knew she was going to find it difficult to sleep that night—she was already excited that her parents were now going to be living with her, never mind this huge surprise. This was definitely a new beginning—and no traditional Christmas this year, her parents had changed all that!

Now they had no time to waste—they were busy with shopping, packing, and reading travel and guide books.

Charlotte was completely buzzing with excitement.

Chapter 17:
The Controlling of a Mind

Anne and Charlotte were now hardly apart from the moment they woke up in the morning, and Charles and Robert settled happily into this new life with the four of them.

Everything was now in place for the trip—dollars had been ordered, and Anne and Charlotte had almost packed.

"Robert, could you run me and Charlotte into town, darling? We need to get the last bits for the hand luggage, and I need to pick up your prescription from the chemist."

"Yes, dear, of course, dear!"

Charlotte laughed. She also wanted her father to drive.

She hardly drove now, and usually left her car in the garage. It helped to make Robert feel needed too. Robert dropped them off outside the coffee shop and arranged to pick them up in three hours.

"Right, Mum, do you have the list of the final items we need? I cannot believe we are doing this, it feels a little crazy, but I am so excited!"

"I know, darling, in ten days' time we shall be flying, and we shall be in Hollywood! I am excited too, darling—I wonder if we shall see Richard Gere? He was so delightful in Pretty Woman!"

"Really, Mum, wait until I tell Dad! You know how jealous he gets! And, ummm, brownie points for me!"

"You have always been a daddy's girl, you will miss your mum when I am gone!"

Anne looped her arm into Charlotte's.

"Mum, you do make me laugh, you're always saying that you know I love you both equally!"

"I am teasing you, I know you love me, darling!"

Anne and Charlotte walked around the shops together getting everything that was on their list. The joy and love between them were a bond no one could ever break.

"That's it, we are finished, and there's enough time to have another coffee before your father arrives!"

"Mum, we have forgotten Dad's prescription!"

"Good job you remembered, Charlotte! Unless it's on my list I would forget. Your mother's getting old!"

"I don't think so, Mum, you're only 66! That's hardly old."

"Sixty-seven in February, Charlotte, and I shall be seventy soon. How the years have gone by! It catches up on you before you know it!"

Charlotte laughed and they made their way into the chemist. Anne collected Robert's prescription, then told Charlotte she needed to buy some laxatives. Charlotte watched in horror as her mother picked up ten packets from the shelf.

"Mum, you don't need all those! They have 24 in a packet—that lot will last you a year!"

"I do need them, Charlotte. I'm struggling to go to the toilet, darling, and I'm taking eight a day."

"Are you kidding me, Mum? That's not right! How long has this been going on? I am ringing the doctor when we get home!"

"It's fine, I have just adapted to it. I put it down to the stress I was feeling when that letter came. I went to see Dr. Sutherland, and he said it would settle. He prescribed me some laxative medicine, but it didn't work, so I just continued buying these over the counter."

"Mum, taking laxatives on a regular basis is not right! It can cause horrific damage, did you not read the label? It tells you to consult your doctor if the problem persists! Does Dad know what you have been doing?"

"Yes, he has told me to go and see the doctor, because I have a lump in my tummy, and I just call it my apple!"

"That's it, Mum, as soon as we are home, I'm calling our doctor! You need to register anyway now for Dad's next prescription. They will do a proper health check-up."

"OK, darling, if it keeps you happy!"

Robert arrived to collect them, and Charlotte immediately began questioning her father regarding this, asking why he had not done anything to sort it. He just said that Charlotte knew how strong and resilient her mother was, and that she would only do what she wanted to do.

When they arrived home, Charlotte dumped her bags and immediately rang her surgery, saying that they were going away on holiday soon and this matter needed to be dealt with immediately.

The nurse made an emergency appointment with Dr. Collins for 8.30 in the morning. Charles told Charlotte to ease up on her mother—she was only doing what she thought was right and had never been a frequent visitor to the doctor anyway.

Robert drove Charlotte and her mother to the surgery, arriving early so that they could register her, and she would be on the system.

Anne described all her systems and explained her reasons for taking the laxatives. She then mentioned her lump, explaining her pet name for it was "The Apple."

Dr. Collins called for a nurse, saying he wanted to examine Anne so that he would have a clearer picture.

He asked for Charlotte and her father to wait outside whilst they examined her. Dr. Collins also asked her more detailed questions whilst they were out of the room in case, she wanted to tell him anything in private.

"Ouch, ooh, ouch!"

"That hurts, Mrs. Hughes?"

"Yes, Doctor, it's painful!"

Dr. Collins had his suspicions, but a specialist was needed, along with a series of hospital tests, which he was going to arrange as soon as possible.

Anne looked shocked and so did Robert when he heard what the doctor had to say. They had thought he would say she needed stronger laxatives, but this wasn't the case.

"Dr. Collins, we are going on holiday soon, and there is still so much to do! Will I be able to go? I don't understand the urgency?"

"Mrs. Hughes, the doctors will run the necessary tests. We need to get it sorted for you."

"It will be fine, Mum, at least we can get to the bottom of it, and then you won't have the pain and the problems. I cannot believe you kept this secret!"

"It's not the type of thing you want to discuss, Charlotte, it's embarrassing and even the examination was very intrusive!"

"I understand, Mum. You OK, Dad?"

The doctor arrived with the paperwork and said he would be in contact, and they were to try not to worry.

Hopefully, by tomorrow, they have the answers to what had been going on. Charlotte phoned to tell Charles the news, and Robert called at the house for some items for Anne's hospital stay.

When the consultant came to see Anne, he examined her thoroughly and ordered blood tests, X-rays, and a CT scan. He arranged for her to have an enema and then a colonoscopy.

"Mr. Williamson, do you have any idea what is wrong with my wife?"

"Mr. Hughes, there are many things that can be the cause, but I would rather wait until we have all the results."

"Thank you on behalf of my wife for all the tests, at least now she isn't dealing with this alone and in secret!"

"Mr. Hughes, when people have problems with their bowels, many people like your wife try to ignore the symptoms and brush it off because of embarrassment. It's why bowel cancer is so high, due to people ignoring the symptoms until it's too late. If treatment commences early, the fatality rate is much lower."

"Are you testing my wife for cancer, Doctor? I am worried now!" Robert's face turned white as fear took hold of him.

"Yes, we are, but we would test anyone with the symptoms your wife has, and until we have the test results,

I cannot give you any more information. Please try not to worry. I know and completely understand your fears and anxiety. I would not like to unduly cause you to stress, but yes, it could be."

Anne completed all the tests, drawing deep into her inner self for a guard of armor to wrap around her body, and her heart and mind.

Charlotte, Charles, and Robert stayed by her bedside until the nurse told them to leave and come back in the morning when the colonoscopy was scheduled.

Robert was a lost soul, with his mind and heart totally crushed. Charlotte's own heart had opened. Pain was beginning to weep from her heart, and she watched as her father quietly headed to his bedroom. She knew it was impossible for her to heal his pain.

Charlotte heard her father during the night, tossing and turning, up and down, almost the whole night. He would be exhausted at the hospital, but he didn't care.

"Ready, Dad, come on, let's get this over with! We shall get Mum well again. Once they know what is wrong with her, then we can deal with it. Mum will not be happy if she finds out you were worrying and hadn't slept, Dad!"

"I am ready. Well, no, actually, I am not ready, Charlotte. I just don't know what I would do if I lost her, I can't control it, Charlotte!" as his body collapsed into hers, desperately seeking strength from his daughter, as she held him tightly in her arms.

"Come on, Dad! I need you to dig really deep, and to breathe, and to be ready for whatever the outcome will be. We are here as a family, and we will get through this. We have been through so much and survived, and we do not know that it is actually cancer! It could be a multitude of things!"

Charles, Charlotte, and Robert arrived on the ward, and could already detect the nurses' looks of sorrow toward them, even though they hadn't been formally told anything. The nurses were awaiting their arrival to page Mr. Williamson immediately.

The family entered the sideward, where they were greeted by Anne's smile. She was in a positive mood, joking as usual, as the nurse brought in a tray of tea behind them.

"Look, only the best for your mother, Charlotte! They have given us their finest china!"

"Mum, honestly, only you, Hyacinth!"

Robert kissed his wife and sat in the chair by her bed, as Charles poured the tea.

Charlotte could see that her mother had been crying.

Anne had fixed her face with makeup, trying desperately to cover up her pain. As Charlotte passed her mother a cup of tea, she burst into tears, she just could not hold it in any longer. Charlotte knew her mother had cancer, and that she was going to die. Her heart was bursting inside. She knew that she had been given a gift, the power to see know about the future. It was a power that many people would love to have, so that they would be able to prepare their hearts, in the light of such a warning.

This time, it was a gift Charlotte wished she had never had. She didn't want to know, she wanted hope. In her heart, though, she knew that what she wanted would be nothing more than a miracle.

For during the previous night, Charlotte had been forewarned. In the middle of the night, her familiar ghosts had appeared, pulling at her bed covers, and stroking her face. Charlotte was initially resilient, fighting hardback at them, but they would not leave. She knew she had to listen. Charlotte wouldn't be given a second chance if she didn't manage to stay strong.

Otherwise, she knew without a doubt, that she would be unable to walk back again through the door to her father and Charles.

"Charlotte! It's time! It's your mother's time!"

Suddenly Luke appeared, standing by the ghost's side with Jacob in his arms.

"Sissy, it's time for you to make mother ready for her journey back to God. It's Jacob's time, Sissy, time for him to be back in our mother's arms. Just like it will be for Courtney when your time comes to hold her again. I have cradled Jacob in my arms, and settled his cries for mother, helping him to settle in heaven, and awaiting her time. You have to help Mother to come now. It's her time, Sissy, and as hard as it is for you, Mother will need your hand to guide her to us. She needs to follow the light, and we shall be waiting. She needs to come soon, otherwise, she risks being stuck between two worlds. We shall find her peace, Sissy, and you know that mother has always protected you. You now need to be strong for her, and to let her know she will be at peace here."

"Please, Luke, there has to be another way! I'm begging you, Luke!"

Luke began to sing, "Hush, now, Sissy, please don't cry, Mother's always going to love you, even when she dies."

"No, Luke, please! No, I can't let her go, I won't be able to survive!"

"Sissy, it will be shown to her as it was to you. If Mother chooses to come back, if she sees you at the window, you have been forewarned of the consequences! If she tries to come back to your world, her soul will be lost and stuck in between the two worlds. What do you think will happen, Sissy, if your time arrives and Mother's not here? What then, Sissy? Where will you go? Your soul would be desperately searching for Mother! That would mean two beautiful souls lost, and all God's teachings would have come to nothing! I am here, Sissy, with our Jacob, and together we shall help show mother where to go. Even so, she needs your help to cross over! We love you, Sissy!"

Suddenly, they disappeared. Luke and Jacob had gone!

Charlotte was sobbing as she felt Charles's arms holding onto her. Charles had entered the room at an earlier point and heard her side of the conversation. He knew that she was talking to the ghosts of her beautiful brothers. He had heard her desperate, one-sided pleas not to take her mother from her. Charlotte was now begging for more time. Charles watched helplessly as his wife sobbed. All he could do was hold her, as the spirits left and sent her back to his arms.

Charles knew that this must have been a warning of the tragedy that was to come. This would be the worst devastation for both Charlotte and Robert, and Charles knew that he was going to have to fight and protect them with all his inner strength.

"Now, we are to have no tears, do you hear me, Charlotte?"

Sitting around Anne's bedside, Robert cried into his hands, while Charles kissed Anne and held Charlotte.

193

Anne reached for Robert's hand as she fought back her own tears.

Mr. Williamson took a deep breath as he entered the room and told them as steadily as possible, that unfortunately, Anne had bowel cancer. Furthermore, it had broken into the stomach where it had masticated from the bowel through to the liver. He advised them that they would be holding a team meeting later that afternoon to see if there was anything that could be done.

He informed them that the hospice and Macmillan nurses would be in shortly to offer any help with questions, and to tell them about the support they could offer to Anne and her family.

He ended by saying that he regretted to inform them that their holiday would need to be canceled, as Anne was no longer fit to fly.

After the team meeting, Dr. Williamson arrived back to a room filled with pain, but it was a room in which each of them had been grasping desperately at the faint hope that something might still be done. Dr. Williamson spoke quietly and sincerely, as he delivered the devastating blow. Anne would be dead within a month.

"No, please, you must be able to do something? Please, Doctor, please, you must help my mother!"

Even though Charlotte had been forewarned by her encounter with Luke and Jacob, she still wanted God to grant her a miracle.

Robert collapsed and cried into Anne's arms. Charles held Charlotte tightly, despair running through his veins.

He was desperately worried that this would totally destroy his wife, fearing that this might be a crisis which he was unable to stop, but he knew he would do anything to safeguard her. He saw the pain in both Robert and Anne's eyes at the realization that they were going to be parted by God's hand calling her home.

Charles's mind was going crazy with his own questioning. Surely Anne was too young to die? Robert and Anne should have had years together, they should be growing old together like his own parents had done.

Anne's tears fell as she watched her broken-hearted family. The doctor left the room with tears in his eyes.

"Hello, Anne, are you ready to go home? Are you sure this is what you want? If you would rather go to the hospice, it is not too late to decide."

"I am completely sure, Gillian. I want to spend my last days and every single hour of each of those days with my family."

"Then you will have a support package in place. The Macmillan nurses will sleep each night at your home, Anne, and your GP will call every day, so will the district nurse. Ask them anything. If you need extra support, please don't be afraid to ask any questions. They will do their best to address any areas of concern or anxieties that you might have. I am so sorry for you, and for your family. I don't know where you are getting your strength from. My only regret is that I wish we could have done more for you!"

"That is so kind of you to explain it all again to me, but that is my wish. I wish to go home. I am very grateful for all the support and care I have received from everyone. I cannot thank you all enough; the nurses, for making me laugh, and ensuring I am as comfortable as I can be, when I am in pain. My family will find it difficult trying to control their emotions while trying to keep a smile on my face. I know we will need each other every single minute of every passing day. The hardest part for me, though, is the part when I will have to leave them. I wish I could just take some medicine and go to sleep and never wake up. It would be over and done with quickly.

"I don't want to cause even more pain to them, and I know that my beautiful daughter is going to struggle the most. I also want as much support as possible for my darling Robert. I am praying that he finds the strength and courage to carry on without me. I hope that my words will be enough to get him through the days and let time heal his scars and wounds. I am also very fortunate, Gillian, to have a wonderful son in law called Charles. He will be my rock and will take the lead for the family when I am gone. I have written individual letters for each of them, to be opened after I have passed. Hopefully, these letters will bring them some peace. I know through my passing, I will live on in my daughter. I strongly believe there is another place where we can watch over our loved ones from beyond the beautiful skies.

"I know Charlotte believes this too and that's what I have to remind her. So, Gillian, am I ready? No, but what else can I do? God is calling me home. I shall be with my sons, Jacob and Luke. I know that I'm going to my family in heaven. They have been waiting for me for years. I will walk the stairway to heaven as they reach for me, but I know that as I look back, I have to say goodbye to my Charlotte, and my beautiful husband Robert, and I will need to leave Charles to hold them, as I look on. That's the strength I shall need. The strength to say goodbye."

"Oh, Anne!"

Gillian was crying and just held Anne tightly as she finally broke down and released the tears and the pain and the many worries she had been hiding inside, trying to put on a brave face with a gentle smile, so that her family wouldn't break.

Anne already knew their hearts had been beaten almost to death with a hammer, as the blood wept from within.

How would they ever cope and regain their lives without her? Normality would never exist again for them. They had suffered so much pain as a family in the past, and they knew how to adjust after turmoil, but their grieving would be deep. Each of them had been empowered by her love for so long.

Anne had made a list. She planned to work with Charlotte at her funeral. She knew that Robert wouldn't be able to cope, and even Charles, as strong as he was, would struggle. There was no doubt that it would have to be Charlotte. This would be the hardest thing she would ever have to ask Charlotte to do in her entire lifetime, and she needed to help her through it as much as she could. Anne knew that Charlotte would follow it through—in fact, she knew Charlotte would do anything for her, but she had had her mother's support to help with her grief before, and this would be the last time Anne could protect her on the terrestrial plane.

Even at this stage of her life, the worst thing for Anne was that if she had known she was going to die, she would have wanted to die in her own home and would never have sold it and moved away.

Robert, Charles, and Charlotte brought Anne back to the house, and the afternoon passed as if time has pushed the accelerator button. The clouds passed by so quickly that the world seemed to be spinning faster and faster, as if on a mission of destruction.

Chapter 18:
Anne's Final Journey

Anne was overwhelmed by the flowers, cards, and the numerous visitors who came by to show their love and support.

Anne was becoming weaker now. Two weeks had passed, and time was against her. Charlotte was completely exhausted. Her heart was overwhelmed with pain, grief ripping through her as it tried to take control of her body again. Her mind was screaming out for everyone to leave them alone. Charlotte would fall asleep crying into Charles's arms as he tried to get her to rest. She was heading back to where she had fallen before, over-emotional and exhausted.

She had watched her father holding her mother all day and all night, and she had told Robert not to leave her side. Anne had been having panic attacks and hallucinations, and she was frightened and scared. These finally began to settle when the doctor increased her medication. Robert's own appetite had gone, and he was surviving mostly by drinking tea, as Anne's last few days dawned.

The Macmillan team and the hospice coordinators kept in daily contact with each other, and before long they decided that it was time to say no more visitors.

Hard as it was to tell people, they now needed this personal time as a family to express their love. They had to prepare themselves for Anne's final hours.

"Charlotte, come and lay with me, darling!" Anne's body was now deteriorating rapidly, much faster than Dr. Williamson had expected. She was drifting into a deep sleep, as the needle in her arm delivered the drugs to her body. Her GP had been increasing the dose daily. He had wanted her to have no pain—that was the one and only thing she had asked from him, please, no pain.

While they had been making arrangements for her funeral, Anne had told Charlotte the full story about the events that had taken place when Jacob had been born.

Anne wanted to go back to God with her conscience clear, and she needed Charlotte's promise that she would not punish Robert for it but would love him even more.

Anne explained that it had been an argument that should never have taken place, and her father was never to be blamed, ever, for the loss of Jacob. Anne made it clear that she had long ago forgiven him, as he had forgiven her for her original mistrust in him. It had been one second in their lives which had had dreadful consequences—a second that could not be changed, but one that Robert had carried that weight of for his entire life. He still mourned Jacob every day.

Charlotte understood and accepted what her mother had requested. She knew that her father was not a wife-beater, and he was certainly not a murderer. Robert would never have hurt his wife intentionally, nor any of his children.

Anne asked Charlotte to watch over Robert, saying she should encourage him to live again after she had gone.

Anne knew that he had always been in love with her and had never broken his wedding vows. His solemn vow had always been until death do us part. When they had been making arrangements for her funeral. Anne said that she wanted a white American casket with a crucifix on the top, with the handles, etc. all in silver. White flowers were to be placed only in the church and on top of her casket, and mourners could send flowers as long as they were white. Red roses were only to be sent by her immediate family. She wanted to be dressed all in white, and to have with her, her rosary beads, her bible, and the individual letters which had been written to her by Robert, Charlotte, and Charles.

Anne promised Charlotte that she would give her a sign to let her know that she had arrived safely in heaven, telling her that she would always watch over her. She told Charlotte, "God forbid, if anyone hurts you, I will scare them to death in the middle of the night!"

She reminded Charlotte that she would only be gone from her sight. The nurse checked her pulse as she lay dying. Suddenly she called out for Luke and Jacob to take her hand and they appeared before her. Charlotte screamed and Charles held on tightly to her as Anne passed, to the sound of screams from both Charlotte and her father.

A beautiful funeral was held for Anne, and she was laid to rest next to Luke's grave. Her body was gone from sight, but her soul would live on. Charlotte would always remember the day she died, the 16th of January 2015.

Now Charlotte waited at her window, hoping a miracle would be granted, and her mother would return.

Charles had bought an apartment at the beach for them to live in. He didn't want Charlotte to live in the big house any longer, and this was his plan to save her.

Hoping and praying as she watched the tide, that it would heal her grief. Charlotte now felt she had no reason to live, could she herself find a reason, or would the pain of grief and fate finally take its toll. Would Charles's love save her? Could Charlotte find the strength to walk again and continue the legacy of The Red Shoes as she "waits for the tide?"

The End